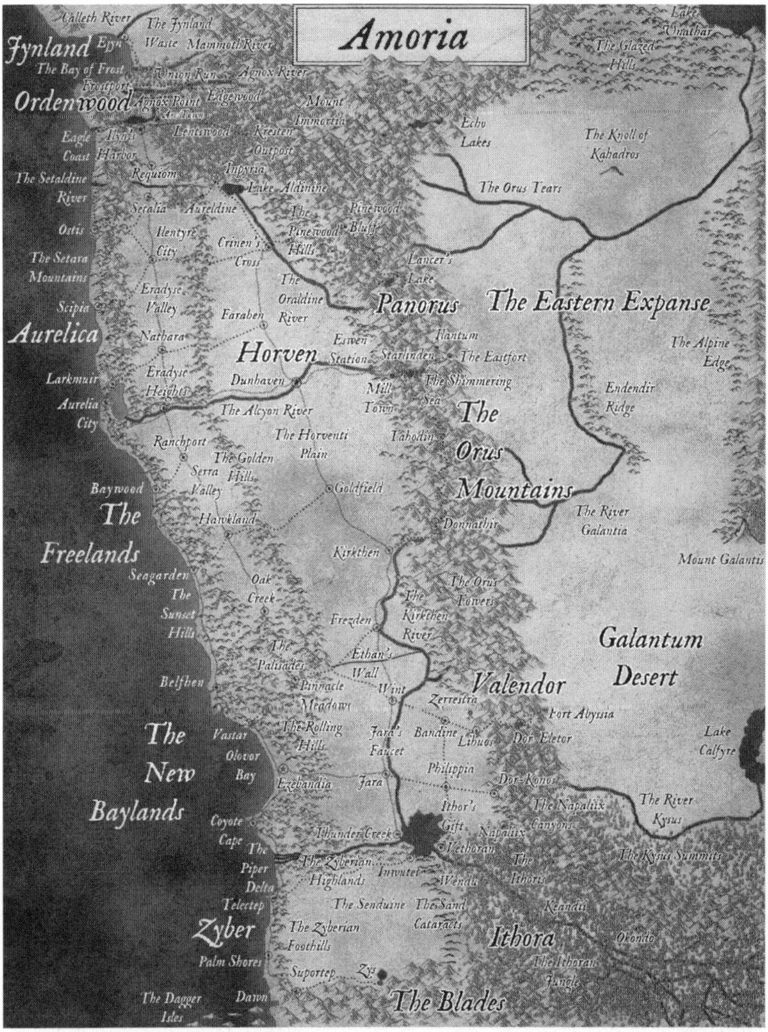

Light and Shadow

The Revenge of the Forsaken

Denis Shanagher

Copyright © 2022 by Denis Shanagher

All rights reserved.

No part of this publication may be reproduced, stored or transmitted in any form or by any means, electronic, mechanical, photocopying, recording, scanning, or otherwise without written permission from the publisher. It is illegal to copy this book, post it to a website, or distribute it by any other means without permission.

Contents

1. A Faceless Shadow — 1
2. Fear and Friendship — 9
3. Rise to Command — 35
4. Peace or Glory — 44
5. The Board is Set — 51
6. An Eastern Escape — 59
7. History Returns — 69
8. Valendor's Deception — 75
9. A Sight Unseen — 80
10. Xastix's Cradle — 87
11. The Mist — 92
12. Moving Pieces — 114
13. Zila's Gambit — 118
14. Foe and Friend — 128
15. Ruin — 143
16. The Turn of the Tide — 157

17. Under Fire and Mountain	164
18. The Mirage of Suportep	171
19. Limited Power	184
20. A Dissemination of Strength	193
21. Implacable	197
22. A Shadow in Dying Light	201
23. Fractured Lines	216
24. Shattered Future	220

1

A Faceless Shadow

The sun is setting on Amoria. The day's light has already fallen behind the towering Orus Mountains, casting a great shadow on the plains of the Eastern Expanse. The burning beacon atop the Eastern Eye, a skyscraping stone watchtower jutting from the steep mountainside, is now more visible than ever, but nevertheless, Tharmir does not slow his steed. Several members of his scouting party are beginning to fade, and he needs to alert Captain Ben of his group's tribulations.

From way atop the watchtower, the obscured figures can finally be seen approaching. A bellowing horn is blown to alert the Eastfort of the party's return.

Svender Ben, Captain of the Eastfort, is relieved to hear of Tharmir's arrival. His scouting party was scheduled to be back four days ago, and the party's tardiness is the first exciting thing to happen during Ben's captaincy at the fort. He is anxious to find out what caused such an unexpected disturbance in their otherwise undisturbed normalcy. Down to his left, Captain Ben can see seven riders returning from his vantage atop the fort, less than half of those who rode out weeks ago.

The party rides from the expanse into the Panorum Gate, the unique wide gap piercing the steep slopes of the Orus Mountains. Across the range, it is the only valley connecting to the Eastern Expanse for hundreds of miles.

The party is out of both food and water, and rides with brittle haste. Indeed, as they take a right turn back into the Eastfort gate, two riders collapse from their horses onto the stone streets. As composed as he can be, Tharmir instructs nearby soldiers to escort all but one of his party to the infirmary.

The Eastfort is a historic fort built—or some might even venture to say carved—of gray stone into the backside of a mountain. It overlooks the Orus Pass, a valley road which leads all the way west through the mountains to the capital of the Kingdom of Panorus, Starlinden. It has two twenty-foot-tall walls, one on its outskirts and the other on the inside, splitting the fort between its upper and lower sections. Vertical steps bisect the fort from its gate to its top, while also connecting to its few horizontal roads.

Tharmir and one accompanying rider from his party dismount their horses in the courtyard behind the gate, round a command tower, and weakly climb the stone steps to the main hall of the keep at the top of the fortress. This part of the fort is truly built into the mountain itself, as only the front arches remain outside.

Once they enter, Captain Svender Ben, surrounded by other scouting leaders stationed at the fortress, greets the two with a serious tone. "Leader Tharmir, your belated return is of great concern to me. What unexpected trouble has befallen your party?"

Tharmir answers defeatedly with a hint of fear. "Captain, the failure of the party is mine. We have ventured too far in our mission and seen what we should not have seen."

The hall is dark. Only a few lamps line the walls of the cavernous room, with the rest of the light coming from the evening sky peeking through the hall's open doors. There is little wind at the base of these mountains, but a cool, crisp air still fills the room.

Ben presses Tharmir. "Are you saying that your party exceeded your mandate? You explored past your route?"

"I am afraid so, and the repercussions have been levied upon us."

"I expected more control from a man of your experience. You have been leading scouting runs for over twenty years. A true grizzled veteran of the Eastfort, and supposedly my most trusted leader. What happened?"

"A discovery we didn't plan for on the edge of our route... in the northern hills of Mount Galantis itself. We found an anomaly. An impossible forest—old and thick, while being much within the volcano's fiery range. Our route nearly touched its border, so I ordered an investigation. For a few days, we would ride into the forest and study its composition."

"And what is it you found?"

"It's hard to explain. The air in the forest was thin, and a faint voice could be heard... almost calling to us."

Ben is concerned with this report, but more so with the sanity of Tharmir than the reality of these claims. "What did the voice say?"

"I don't know. It was speaking faintly and in a foreign language, although it was reminiscent of the Autoch-speech."

"Are you certain of this?"

"No, I am unsure. It has been years since I have heard the dialect."

"So, then what happened? Why is half of your party missing?"

"On the last day of extra scouting, I ordered a group farther in than before, just to set a longer eastern scouting border."

"You did this despite hearing voices?"

"We were unsure if we were hearing voices coming from the forest. The thought that we could be hearing them was considered impossible; there had to be a logical explanation." He pauses and sighs, breaking eye contact for a moment before continuing. "That group never returned, so I sent the whole party after them, assuming they got lost. But, as we ventured further into the forest, a dry mist surrounded us and became thicker and thicker... Before I knew it, we had been enveloped by this fog. Visibility was below three feet. I ordered a retreat, but we were disoriented. We had already stretched the trip out and were low on supplies, so we needed to escape. It took us three days to navigate our way out, and in the process of doing so we lost, literally speaking, three of our party."

"How is that possible?"

"One minute they were there, and the next, they were gone. We couldn't see a thing."

"They didn't call out for you?"

"We never heard from them again." Tharmir paused, remorsefully thinking of his lost companions. "If we had not found Sedgen here, we all probably wouldn't have made it." He gestures over to his scout.

Captain Ben looks over to the young man next to Tharmir. The soldier is hardly over twenty, and has a malnourished physique with scars across his skin. "Are you okay? You look like a ghost."

"I'm just a little lightheaded, that's all," Sedgen stammers, his stare practically blank.

Tharmir continues anxiously. "Sedgen was in the party I sent on the last day. We found him unconscious on the forest floor on the third day of our search. He had managed to climb one of the tall trees and see the edge of the forest, but had been knocked out for an unknown amount of time due to lack of food and water."

"What happened to your group, Sedgen?"

Sedgen tries to speak but, all he can do is stutter, looking more ill than before. He gives a look of confusion and frustration mixed with fear.

"This man is seriously unwell," Ben states. "We need to get him to the infirmary."

"Hold on; you need to hear what happened. I'll try to help by telling you what he told me. He said the group saw someone in the distance—a hooded figure."

Sedgen is now shaking, but through his struggling, he manages a nod in agreement.

"They followed it in secret, and they saw signs of activity—trees cut, lots of footprints in the ground."

Sedgen stops shaking, his stare remains blank, but he finally seems to be calm and under control.

"Finally, they crested a small hill and found an opening in the forest. That's when they saw it."

"Saw what?"

Tharmir looks over to Sedgen, who is now staring directly at him, wondering if he wants to speak. Sedgen's stare remains blank, and after a few moments, Tharmir continues. "They saw…"

"No!" Sedgen interjects menacingly.

Tharmir turns and looks confused. Then, in one swift motion, Sedgen draws his sword and thrusts it upwards through Tharmir's stomach and out his upper back.

Tharmir is paralyzed in shock. He gasps for air, but he cannot find any. The other scouting leaders in the room draw their guns immediately.

"No, don't kill him! We need him alive!" Ben exclaims while gesturing his hands into the air.

Sedgen pushes Tharmir away while sliding his sword out, and Tharmir collapses to the ground limp. Sedgen turns to the men holding their guns aimed at him. His face shows shock and confusion.

"Take him!" Ben commands in a panic.

Sedgen's face becomes blank again. He flips the blade on himself and deftly slides it into his own chest as the other scouting leaders approach him. He instantly slumps face-first to the ground.

Everyone is frozen in shock and confusion. Thinking quickly, Ben rushes over to Sedgen, flips him over, and removes the sword. "Someone apply pressure to the wound! And Dustin, get a medic!"

Sedgen looks over to Tharmir, whose stunned face is now lifeless, and then turns to see his own wound. He brings his hands in front of his eyes and sees them covered in blood. He, too, now looks shocked and afraid.

"What did you see, Sedgen? What happened to your group!?" Ben asks desperately.

He can see Sedgen's health is failing fast. Sedgen tries to speak but, his mouth is filled with blood. He chokes and desperately grabs Ben, but his grip slowly fails, and he stops breathing.

After a few moments of empty hope for him to return to life, Ben speaks disappointedly. "He's gone."

Ben stands up and looks away at nothing in particular, then back again at the two lifeless bodies in fort's main hall. "What the blaze just happened!?"

He quickly remembers the other scouts. "We need to go to the infirmary immediately and collect statements from the survivors."

Just as he says this, Dustin returns from the infirmary with two medics. Ben greets them with stern urgency while wiping the blood off his hands onto his green cloak. "I am afraid there's nothing more we can do for these two. We need to ensure the survival of the others. It is critically important."

"Captain, all five of the surviving party members have died," Dustin informs him.

"What!? How is this possible?"

One of the medics answers with feigned composure. "The official cause of death is unknown, but they were vomiting blood and exhibiting rash-like burns across their skin. We haven't seen anything like it before. They must have contracted some disease."

"Yet they all died at the same time? That's improbable at best."

"We agree that the circumstances surrounding their deaths are unusual. However, they were all in very poor condition when they arrived."

Ben, trying to remain calm amidst this tragedy, addresses both medics. "I want a full report and autopsy on all seven men. Use your utmost caution and look for anything out of the ordinary, especially with this one here." He says his last sentence while pointing at Sedgen.

The medics give a traditional salute, placing either of their arms at the chest and moving them outward sharply, and then begin to work with some of the leaders to collect the bodies. As they leave, Ben gestures for everyone else to exit as well. The door shuts behind the last of them, leaving him alone in dim lantern light. He walks over to his desk in the corner, which is covered in maps of the eastern frontier, and stops to contemplate his next course of action, shaking what disturbance he can from his thoughts.

He was given command of the Eastfort after years serving in the Panorum military. He's reached this point in his career the hard way, slowly gaining rank and respect through minor victories like settling property disputes and disbanding rogue militias. His latest task is a relatively simple assignment, just sending and monitoring scouting trips in the Eastern Expanse for a few years, but it is a great honor. The Eastfort is considered by all of Amoria to be one of the most important fortresses. It's the front-line of defense against their common enemy, the savage Autoch. To be given this responsibility at his age of thirty indicates his designation as a potential candidate for general upon the task's completion, which also means a failure here, with the world's eye upon him, would doom his aspirations. He knows he must choose his next decision very carefully.

Finally, after some time, he releases a heavy sigh, clears some maps out of the way, and takes a seat at his desk. He grabs parchment and his quill and begins to write.

2

FEAR AND FRIENDSHIP

Prince Niike leans against the fencing of the observation deck of the Ithoran Tree, the great wooden tower and palace of the Ithoran capital, Okondo. It's his favorite spot in the city. He can see all the way across the sunlit jungle to the high Orus Mountains in the north and the steep Blades mountain range in the west.

Okondo, like all Ithoran cities, is unlike all other Amorian cities, and what separates the capital from other Ithoran settlements is its sheer size and the wonder of the Ithoran Tree. Ithoran cities are built upon the jungle they reside in. They are comprised of treehouses connected by rope bridges, along with stilted buildings connected by likewise stilted bridges. Every structure is made from the wood of the jungle's kapok and palm trees. The buildings are built above the ground due to the swamp-ridden floor of the jungle, along with its consistent flooding. In fact, most Ithorans travel by boat from city to city along the Ithoris river, especially if they are headed north with its flow.

Directly in Niike's vision today is, in fact, this great Ithoris river, which winds through the heart of the Ithoran Kingdom. The royal family is expecting rare guests, and he is very excited to meet them. Ithorans rarely get visitors of real importance, as the Ithoran Jungle is hard to navigate, and the kingdom is generally removed from global politics.

Next to Niike is his older brother Silas, his younger sister Kristi, and his old father, King Wisor Chutuluru. They are all dressed in formal Ithoran attire, which entails brightly colored cloth robes over dark cloth shirts and shorts. Wisor's and Silas's robes are yellow, Kristi's are purple, and Niike's are a mix of bright green and blue.

The King sports a more concerned look on his weathered face than Niike's look of anticipation. Today is the expected arrival of the King of Valendor, Hylzar Dumelor, and with him surely comes a proposition that conflicts with the Ithorans' traditional isolationist policies.

"I see them! Over there, on the eastern riverbank!" Niike points.

Wisor nods with a discontented look and moves to descend the tower. His children follow suit. "You seem concerned, father," Silas states inquisitively as the four travel down the many steps.

"Hylzar Dumelor is not to be trusted. He brings us nothing but trouble, as do all outsiders."

Niike speaks confidently. "Why do you fear them so much? I do not see the evil in them, as you do. More interaction with the other kingdoms can bring Ithora more wealth and knowledge."

Wisor shakes his head, annoyed, as he continues to labor downward. "You think you know everything, Niike, and then you spout nonsense such as this. You should know the others seek only to dominate us, as they always have throughout our history in both the old world and the new. The outsiders can only bring us problems. We must protect ourselves, for certainly no one else will. I have accepted Dumelor's request for an audience only out of courtesy. Whatever he offers will be rejected."

***

King Hylzar and his Valendi escorts arrive in Okondo within the hour and head for the five-story palace surrounding the base of the artificial Ithoran Tree. From the ground, the building's architecture is most awe-inspiring. Stilted, like the rest of the buildings in Okondo, the palace rises above the Ithoris itself, as this exact shallow point is the final confluence of several different streams into the major river. It's constructed out of reddish-brown palmwood, much like a pyramid, with tiered levels covered by numerous asymmetrical pitched roofs. After the fifth story, and in the center of the building, the tower that gives the Ithoran Tree its name rises above. Standing roughly 450 feet tall, the square tower is just large enough to fit a single rectangular spiral staircase that leads to its partially covered observation deck, which overhangs off of each side. To reach the palace, bridges jut across the water from the building's east, north, and west sides to the rest of the city.

Hylzar travels with his contingent across the widest northern bridge and through the main palace doors, which are intricately carved with depictions of the founding of the capital. The foreigners are then quickly guided to the candlelit throne room on the first-floor, where Wisor and the rest of the royal family wait, along with several advisors, Inpyrian Knights, and generals.

The Valendi escorts are dressed head-to-toe in the magnetite steel armor unique to their kingdom, for the mountains where they reside are abundant with the ore, and they have become experts at crafting it. It was the reason they initially settled a mining colony there in the first-place long ago. Their armor includes shin-guards, thigh-guards, chest-plates, bracers, shoulder-plates, and helmets with horizontal spaces cut for the eyes and three vertical lines cut near the mouth. From afar, the metal appears black, but when examining closely, one can make out distinctive patterns of flowing black-and-gray banding.

Hylzar himself is an older man, and wears traditional Valendi hooded silk black robes with a white tunic partially showing underneath. These robes have become less prominent in the Valendi culture, as their silk was only able to be collected in the old world. The silk in his robes has to be over 750 years old.

Hylzar enters the high-ceilinged throne room looking confident and imposing amongst the many Ithorans. He directs his attention up at Wisor, whose portly frame sits upon an ornate carved wooden throne, which itself rests on a five-foot high raised platform. The two are roughly the same age, yet Wisor looks far more weathered.

"Greetings, King Wisor. It is a great pleasure to finally meet you and to look upon the extraordinary Ithoran Tree." Hylzar speaks in a suave tone and sports a calm smile.

"King Hylzar, it is my duty as King of Ithora to welcome all visitors into Okondo and the Ithoran Jungle. It would be a shame never to experience the wonders of our forest kingdom," Wisor responds with a straight face.

"Well, you are certainly right about the beauty of your jungle. I am in awe with every step I take."

"You are very gracious, King Hylzar... Now, tell me, what prompted you to make this trip?"

Hylzar's expression turns to one of composed concern. "Unfortunate circumstances, I'm afraid. Circumstances that I figured must be discussed in person, given their gravity—A great evil stirs in the north."

"Are you referring to your own kingdom's rapid rise in military production and power? I have heard your magnetite mines have doubled their production capacity, and your black-powder reserves swell."

The jibe doesn't appear to affect Hylzar. "King Wisor, you of all people are aware of the importance of self-preservation. It is the very reason I have come here. My actions have been forced, and I am afraid my efforts are no longer enough to keep peace in the region. Queen Korza Amoria and her Baylanders seek finally to reestablish themselves as the great power they once were in the old world."

Wisor is dismissive. "There is no proof to these allegations. The Baylanders have been a peaceful kingdom for a century."

"Yes, but can you not see what is happening? Korza has raised an army unprecedented in Amoria's history. Thousands of troops and siege weapons are added to her force every month. And, unfortunately, I'm afraid our problems only get worse—I have been informed that the young and ambitious Queen of Zyber, Zila Sumptet, has allied with Korza in secret. The motivation behind the move being an agreement to divide the conquered Ithora in two by the Ithoris river. In exchange, Zila will commit her forces to the Baylander army to completely wipe out the last remnants of the once-great Kingdom of Valendor."

"And what, would you say, would motivate such an act of unprompted aggression?" Wisor responds in a still-unconvinced tone.

"I myself pondered this. The likely answer? More greed from the people who betrayed my great kingdom all those years ago. The Baylanders and the Zyberians no longer wish to trade for our metals, wood, and stone. They would rather spill blood and enslave the survivors than spend coin for the hard-earned bounty of our lands. The New Baylands is overpopulated; its demand for the resources that they themselves cannot provide is choking its economy. While in Zyber, there is no wood for building, and hardly any land for farming, thus restricting their own economic growth... They will cut the Ithoran Jungle to the ground if it gets them ahead in this world. The Baylanders and the Zyberians will finish what they started in old world."

"Alright, you have made your argument. Now, get to your purpose here: What do you propose?"

"The Valendi and the Ithorans must move to form an alliance immediately. We will gather our strength in secret near Ithor's Gift, and then, when we are ready, we will move on the offensive in Zyber. With the Valendi protecting your northern flank, Ithora will conquer Zyber's northern cities and push along the Zyberian Highlands to the coast. Once we reach the ocean, you will move south around the Senduine and finish the Zyberians by taking their capital, Suportep. Zyber will fall before the Baylanders can mobilize their forces to break my Valendi defensive position, and they will now be surrounded by rivals—Valendor and Ithora below, and the northern kingdoms above. Their borders are too large to defend against so many foes."

Once he is sure Hylzar is finished, Wisor gives a long sigh. The rest of the room remains silent for some time while he musters his response. "King Hylzar, you ask much of me and my people, and expect us to take you on your word. I have heard of no such alliance, and I will not so freely commit my people to bloodshed against stronger adversaries. That being said, I will honor your proposition with a discussion with my council, and will give you word on my decision tomorrow... In the meantime, as is proper in our culture, I will provide you and your companions food and shelter. My head servant, Master Copa here, will show you to your abodes. Please accept my invitation for supper tonight."

Dumelor, as calm and collected as ever, responds. "I graciously accept your offer. Thank you for your audience, King Wisor."

Hylzar exits the throne room confidently under the suspicious gaze of Wisor. As soon as the doors are shut behind the Valendi King and his followers, Wisor speaks. "What nonsense he delivers us. A false alliance and a feigned attempt to create fear amongst our people for his own gain. It is the Valendi who wish to be the conquerors... the revengers. He moves to use our people as fodder for his own conquests."

"I agree this is likely the case, but even so, we should investigate his allegations. Send a message to Suportep to contact our network there. If the alliance is true, we would be at great risk," General Ikano, the veteran leader of the Ithoran army, advises the king.

"Very well—only because it's easy—but I will not be made a fool by Dumelor. I will reject his proposal tomorrow and send him on his way."

One of the Inpyrian Knights, Sir Inir Avolo, then speaks. "The Inpyrians on the council agree. We know Dumelor better than anyone. He is a shady figure. His rise to power in Valendor has always been mysterious, and his actions while an active member of the Inpyrium were suspect at best. His obsession with Valendi history and his quest for the Ancients' powers concerned his teachers and had him wandering east of the Orus mountains for years before he joined the Valendi council. And don't even get me started on his bastard children."

"And what if he speaks the truth?" Niike asks.

"Then we are endangered," Wisor answers. "Even a combined Valendi and Ithoran power will struggle to stand up to the might of the New Baylands. We have neither the soldiers nor the technology to defeat them; only to outlast them. But, remember that this is hypothetical. The world never has and never will seek to tame the Ithoran Jungle, nor does it have reason to. The effort would do much more harm than good. We are safe here as long as we remain here. This royal meeting is adjourned."

***

Later that night, a massive feast is prepared. The Ithoran hospitality continues as Wisor tries to appease his Valendi neighbors before his announcement of their rejection tomorrow. The dinner occurs in a long dining hall built high in the trees and large enough to sit a hundred guests.

It's Ithoran tradition that there is open seating at official dinners so that anyone can sit with anyone. The royal family separates themselves amongst the many tables so guests can have a better chance to sit with royalty.

When Hylzar and the rest of the Valendi arrive, everyone expects him to sit next to Wisor, so that he may press him with more cunning rhetoric. He walks up to the Ithoran King and greets him. "King Wisor, I can't thank you enough for your hospitality. My treehouse has a stunning view of the city of Okondo, and I already know this meal is going to be terrific, based on the rumors that have proliferated through all of Amoria."

"Thank you, King Hylzar. I have great hope it will live up to the stories."

"I see what I heard was true—no assigned seating here. It's a very interesting way of dining; something I should consider when I return to Valendor." Dumelor is quiet for a moment as he scans the room. "I must follow tradition. I will split my people at each table. I am sure some of my soldiers would love to dine with a king. I wish you a pleasant meal."

And, in a surprising move, Hylzar speaks with his escorts and then sits at a different table. It's one of the younger tables, with most sitting there being in their late teens, including Prince Niike. Wisor lets out a suspicious grunt and takes his seat.

"Come, now. I wish to probe the minds of the Ithoran youth. Tell me about yourselves," Dumelor says to his fellow young diners with a grin.

Wisor is confused by the move, but happy that his meal will not be tarnished with political squabbling. As the courses are served and the drinks are poured, he begins to relax and just enjoy the feast. He watches Hylzar, who is consistently laughing and joking with the rest of his company, from afar from time to time.

Niike is ecstatic that Hylzar sat down at his table. This kind of interaction with a foreigner of such prominence is unheard of in

Ithora. He presses King Hylzar on all sorts of questions around Inpyrians, Valendi history, leadership, and more, and Hylzar is more than happy to indulge him.

As the dinner concludes and people slowly trickle out of the dining hall, Hylzar gets up, again thanks the King, and then thanks his table for the "wonderful company."

However, before he can exit, Prince Niike approaches him. "King Hylzar, you were a pleasure to speak with tonight. It is a shame our dinner did not last longer. It's not often I get to hear such stories and perspectives from outsiders."

"Great to meet you, Prince Niike. You remind me a lot of my younger self." Hylzar then grabs Niike's shoulders. "I wish you great fortune if we do not see each other again. However, something tells me this will not be our last conversation."

And, with that, he leaves.

Niike retires to his room in the palace for the night, his mind lost in thought about his experience with Dumelor. *He clearly is not the evil man that the others have claimed, and if he is not evil, then are his proclamations about the coming war true?*

***

Trees and houses burning and falling left and right. People screaming everywhere. Bodies floating in the swamp below the city of Okondo. Fires raging on the Ithoris itself.

Niike looks out from the palace in despair. Baylander and Zyberian forces have overwhelmed the Ithoran army, and are now killing everything in their path.

He hears shots fired downstairs in the palace and he rushes down. He looks for his family, but they are nowhere to be found.

General Ikano frantically greets him outside the throne room. "Niike, the city is overrun. Our armies are defeated. You need to leave now."

Niike is confused, but nods in agreement. He rushes to his room to find his beloved Iawora in a panic. "Everyone is dying, Niike. Smoke fills my lungs. I'm scared, Niike," she cries.

"We need to get out of the city," he responds.

Niike grabs her and they start running through the palace halls. There is now fighting all around them. Shots whiz past the two as they head for the east door. Once they reach it, they find Zyberian soldiers blocking it off. Niike shoots and kills the three soldiers, while they miraculously miss him.

"Hurry!" he says as he and Iawora sprint for the door.

Just as they are escaping, shots ring out from the other end of the hall. Iawora lets out a loud scream and falls outside onto the wooden palace deck. Niike looks on in horror to see her bleeding profusely from her chest. He grabs her and carries her in a panic across one of the palace's east bridges and sets her behind a tree.

"No, no, no, no, no... You're okay. I'll make it better," he says as he looks at her wound. He tries to stop the bleeding, but it is out of control. "You can't die... I can't live without you."

Iawora raises her bloodied hand to Niike's cheek and struggles to speak. "Niike, I'm sorry. I-I love you."

And, with those words, she passes.

"Nooo!" he yells in despair and hugs Iawora, beginning to cry.

He hears a sound behind him and quickly turns to see a Baylander soldier pointing his pistol directly at him. With a loud bang, the muzzle flashes.

Niike wakes up, sweating and out of breath. His heart is racing. Outside his window, he can see the sun has risen. It cuts through the shading canopy with shards of light hitting both the forest floor and his own bedroom's back wall.

What a horrid dream, he thinks to himself as he looks over to his bed to see the young and angelic Iawora still sleeping peacefully beneath their covers.

Niike rolls out of bed wearing only shorts. His muscular physique is unmatched by those his age, and that, combined with his tall stature, makes him an imposing figure to all Ithorans and the favorite prince of the Ithoran women.

Iawora only adds to Niike's mystique. Even from a young age, her beauty was undeniable, and with that beauty has come popularity. Iawora quickly has become a flagbearer of Ithoran commoners, as the story of her journey from being a poor orphan in Vethoran to a plutocrat in Okondo, all through her work as an influencer of Ithoran culture and commerce, has vaulted her to divine status amongst the people. Her and Niike's reputations caught each other's wind, and the two were instantly a perfect match. When the relationship between them was discovered, it's safe to say Ithorans were all envious of their bond. Who knows how long the relationship will last, though? King Wisor is strongly against it, given Niike's duties as a member of the royal family to marry diplomatically, and his distaste with Iawora herself due to her undignified background.

Niike tries to shake his dream as he puts on his royal garb and heads for the throne room. The King will announce his decision soon, and he wants to see Hylzar again. He arrives to find his father deep in conversation with Sir Numenkor, who is Ithora's highest-regarded Inpyrian Knight, as well General Ikano and his scrawnier older brother Silas.

"Father, what's happening? Where is Hylzar?" Niike asks.

"The decision has been delayed. Coincidentally, a boat came in the night bearing a message from our informants in Zyber. Though it has not been confirmed, there is serious reason to believe the validity of King Hylzar's claims that the Zyberians have allied with the Baylanders. Apparently, Queen Korza just recently visited Suportep in secret. Our sources say she left satisfied, and that as we speak, Queen Zila is likely preparing to announce the alliance formally."

"Then we must side with Hylzar. What we fear is true," Niike responds confidently.

"There is still much to discuss and consider."

"Time is of the essence. We cannot delay and let the Zyberians move first against us."

"The motivations behind this alleged alliance are still unknown. Now, if you will excuse us, the wiser men must deliberate."

"Father—"

Wisor, now irritated, interrupts his son. "You will learn your place and not question my judgment, child. You're evidently ignorant of the many issues at hand. I will not be given orders by my teenage son. Now get out of here."

Niike frustratedly bows and exits. The combination of this news and his dream has him disturbed like never before. He moves to return to his place of solace, the Ithoran Tree. The arduous climb allows him to burn off some steam, but when he completes the journey to the top, he is surprised to find Dumelor himself there, without any guards, taking in the view.

The Valendi King greets him warmly. "I came up here after my meeting with your father was abruptly canceled. I thought I might find you. You mentioned how much you loved it up here last night." Dumelor pauses for a few more seconds to focus on the view. "I can now see why. The way the sun shines on the jungle below really brings calmness and beauty to this world, even in the face of so much turmoil."

Niike, still worked up from his argument with his father, responds. "My father is a fool for not trusting you. I probably shouldn't tell you this, but we got word this morning that the Zyber-New Baylands alliance is true, just as you claimed."

"Ah, I expected as much. Better now than later, though. There is still time to act, even if that time is running out."

"I cannot explain their mistrust of you. Or I am a blind fool?"

Dumelor gives a reassuring smile to Niike. "My reputation is a difficult thing to explain. It doesn't help that I am a Valendi, but it's actually my tragedies that are likely to blame... Let me tell you what happened.

"Long ago, I was just like you—a middle child in a royal family. Selfishly, all I wanted in the world was to be king of Valendor. I studied and trained as hard as I could with the hope that my father would pass the crown onto me, rather than my older brother."

Dumelor pauses to laugh, shaking his head. "It was a fool's errand. According to our tradition, my father would literally have had to disown my brother to make me king, and my brother was a great man; he was honorable and wise beyond his years, and surely worthy of the throne himself. So, I got the next best thing and reaped the benefits of all that misguided hard work. I was selected to attend the academy at the Inpyrium. I got to become an Inpyrian Knight.

"Being a Knight was a great life, full of adventure and prominence. After I graduated, I eventually found my way to a famous outpost on the edge of the Orus mountains called the Eastfort, where I spent years scouting the frontier. I walked where no one else had walked, and discovered lands no one had ever seen.

"Scouting back then, however, was extremely dangerous. Scouting parties were frequently set upon by barbaric Autoch clans. I survived some minor attacks, but I had never faced a force like the one that attacked my group in what would become my final mission. My party was slaughtered, but through my Inpyrian skills, I managed to escape. It took me a long time to make it back to Eastfort, and by the time I did, I was mentally broken. The loss of my colleagues and the adversities of my journey weighed heavy on my mind, and I no longer had the stomach for distant exploration.

"I returned home to Valendor to recover, and then accepted a gracious and thoughtful offer from my father to join his royal council. To join the council at such an early age was an honor rarely bestowed in Valendor, even within the royal family.

"My peace did not last, however, for a few years after I joined the council, everyone residing in the royal palace became rapidly ill all at once. It was as if they were all poisoned and I think only survived because I was spending my days at the time traveling on various research missions on behalf of the Inpyrium. The disease they contracted was one that has never been seen before, and our doctors could not find a cure. It was horrid, like their bodies were melting away. It was not long before they all had perished, and I was forced onto the throne."

Hylzar lets out a great sigh. "In the end, I got what I always wanted, but at such horrible cost. Now, all the people of the Kingdom of Valendor are my family, and I will do anything to protect them—to honor the legacy of my own fallen family."

Niike finds new conviction after hearing Dumelor's tale. "I feel the same for the Ithorans. They are all family to me. They have always loved me, even more so than my own family. My father's inaction puts our entire kingdom at risk."

He pauses and stares into the distance, then glances back at Hylzar. "I had a terrible dream last night. Okondo was being sacked by Zyberians and Baylanders. I know it was just a dream, but I swear, no dream has ever felt so real. It was like I was there. I could feel the world around me. I could see gruesome things right before my eyes. It was terrifying. When I was shot, I could feel what it felt like to be shot. Even if it was just for just a brief moment before I woke."

Dumelor suddenly has a very concerned look on his face. He places his left hand on Niike's shoulder and looks him in the eyes. "Niike, this is extremely disturbing. This may not have been a dream, but in fact, a premonition."

"A premonition?"

"I cannot say for certain, but you may have seen into the future. Knights, due to their sharply attuned minds, occasionally have dreams like the one you described. They feel real because they are real, in a way. The world has given you a glimpse into your future, and it can only be changed if you alter your current path."

Niike is now struggling to hide his fear. "But I am not a Knight. How could I have these dreams?"

"You do not have to be a Knight to unlock Ancient power; the Knights are just specifically trained to do so. A man of your thoughtfulness and intelligence could very likely tap into this power, perhaps from an overflowing of emotions and a strong desire to protect his people... You should consult your head Ithoran Inpyrian Knight, Sir Numenkor, about this at once. He will know what to do."

Niike nods and scampers down the tower.

***

Numenkor's middle-age gives him the strength to remain an elite warrior, while also having the experience to be one of the wisest Ithorans. His lauded academic studies around both exotic flora and guerrilla war tactics in the Ithoran Jungle propelled him all the way to his current seat on the King's council. His expertise on two such different subjects is just another example of his eccentric personality, as is his rumored consumption of the psychedelic Ibobo Shroom for both pleasure and academic inspiration.

Niike finds Numenkor in his study as soon as he can and tells him what he told Dumelor.

"Are you certain of this?" Numenkor says with some doubt in his voice.

"Absolutely."

Numenkor, wearing bright-colored green robes, lowers his quill, stands, and walks over to Niike. He places his left hand on his shoulder, as if doing so could somehow read his thoughts. After a few moments, he recoils and strokes his chin as he responds.

"This is highly unusual. One's connection with the energy around them generally takes years of practice to access at this scale. It is, in fact, so difficult that many believe premonitions are Ancient fiction. Especially for a non-Knight, it typically would require another Knight channeling energy through you to have these visions... However, if you indeed had this premonition, I may be able to access it. You see, my young Prince, if a premonition occurs, that means time in this place has been made out of balance. It makes it easier for others to see the event in the time you have seen—a sort of energy portal, if you will. I will meditate on this and hopefully help bring more clarity to the matter. Try to rest easy tonight, Niike. Hopefully, your dream won't happen again, and we can put this silly matter behind us."

Niike thanks Numenkor and exits, but his mind certainly is not at ease. Never has he felt such turmoil. He feels as if it's consuming him.

***

The next morning, Niike rushes to Numenkor's study. He bursts inside and, before Numenkor can get out a word, he speaks.

"I had the dream again, only this time, it started earlier. Once again, my family was nowhere to be found, and this time I was with you. We were fighting side-by-side until we were eventually forced to retreat, and you were killed. Then, I rushed to the top of the Ithoran Tree just before dawn, only to be shot by a Zyberian woman who was covered in both blood and mud."

"Where was I killed?" Numenkor interrupts anxiously, a stark contrast to his tone yesterday.

"Outside the palace on Ikor's Bridge; downed by a Baylander cannon."

Numenkor shows a troubled face. "Your visions are true premonitions. I saw your future last night, at least up until then. That is where I meet my end." He turns to Niike with a stern expression. "We must change the course of fate. We must ally with Dumelor."

"My father won't be convinced. He reiterated again last night that he plans to reject Hylzar's offer."

"Then he must be reasoned with immediately. What does General Ikano think?"

"He is conflicted. At least, he was last night. Sir Numenkor, I can't allow these horrible things to pass. Every night, I see the love of my life die in front of my eyes. I see my people suffer. This future world is one I cannot live in," Niike pleads desperately.

"I agree, Niike. We must speak with General Ikano at once."

***

They find the reserved and unassuming Ikano in his office, mulling troop garrisons and attack plans if they were indeed to invade Zyber. His small stature is compensated for by his astute mind, both as a tactician and leader. Indeed, Ikano's expert understanding of how to inspire others to follow him grants him the unofficial role of Wisor's most trusted advisor.

Numenkor wastes no time addressing him. "General, the fate of Ithora is at stake, for it is foreseen the city will fall. You must help us convince King Wisor to join with Dumelor."

"Foreseen? You mean you had a premonition?" Ikano asks, taken aback. He raises his hand and strokes his graying beard.

"We both did."

Ikano is initially confused that Niike also had a premonition, but certainly trusts Sir Numenkor's counsel. He pauses for a moment of introspection, then lets out a sigh of regret before readdressing his visitors. "Then our worst fears have been realized. If Wisor does not accept the alliance, we may have to take more drastic measures."

"Careful. This course of action could lead us to a very dark place," Numenkor answers seriously. "Treason, no matter how noble, remains illegal... and we will struggle to find ardent supporters. Rest assured, there will be no need for such an extreme move if the three of us come to him in support of Dumelor. He will heed our combined council."

Ikano rises from his desk. "Then we must move quickly. King Wisor plans to summon Hylzar very soon and reject his proposal. If he refuses, I will have to call on our army to intervene."

This statement causes Niike to stress even further. "A military coup? Don't you think—"

Ikano interrupts him as he heads past them to exit. "The kingdom comes first, Niike—above all else, no matter our personal feelings. I'm sure your father believes the same."

Numenkor follows Ikano out of the room, and Niike follows as well. The situation is unravelling before he has time to process it.

The three men immediately head to the palace, where they find King Wisor with his wife and his two other children in the royal dining room. "Niike, you've missed lunch. Why are you always wandering around, chasing admiration?" Wisor scolds, ignoring the other two entrants.

Visibly perturbed, Niike quickly changes the subject. "Father, we've come to stop you before you make a grave mistake."

"Really?" Wisor responds with annoyed, sarcastic shock, still chewing his meal. "And what mistake is that?"

Numenkor intercedes. "My King, Niike and I have had premonitions... Ithora falls to the Baylander and Zyberian force."

"Premonitions?" Wisor responds incredulously. "And you believe this nonsense, Ikano?"

"I trust these men, my king. And, anyways, it makes sense—the alliance is real. Why else would they join together, if not to conquer their foes? The Zyberians barter with little else."

"You three would go against the wise knowledge of your own king and send thousands of Ithorans to their death in the name of hearsay and bad dreams disguised as magic prophecy." Wisor grimaces. "I guess I have discovered that you are all fools... It is a wonder why I let some of you give me council. This ambush disguised as an intervention is over. Now, step aside. I have some news to deliver to the slimy King Hylzar."

Wisor wipes some crumbs from his face as he rises and heads for the door. However, Niike instead steps in front of the king with resolve. "Father, I implore you to reconsider. You will lead Ithora to ruin."

The irritated Wisor is now fuming. "I said step aside, child. You embarrass the royal family with these antics—all brawn and no brain. The people's fraudulent champion, propped up by your own arrogance."

And with that line, Wisor shoves the stronger Niike out of way. The physical aggression catches Niike off-balance, and he stumbles to the ground, his head whiplashing into the floorboards with a cracking thud.

General Ikano cringes at the altercation. He tries to speak, but is interrupted. "I hate you!" Niike yells at his father, still lying on the ground, his hand resting against the injured side of his head, feeling for blood.

Wisor scoffs and turns to walk away. In the moment, Niike is overcome with the horrid memories of his dreams and the fear of losing Iawora. The future haunts his very heartbeat.

He reaches into his holster, pulls out his pistol, and fires.

Niike's emotional rage only lasts long enough to fire just once, but that is all it takes to fell the old king. The bullet rips through Wisor's back and ruptures his heart, ensuring his death.

Various screams can be heard from the royal family, whom have been stunned still, watching with fright as the confrontation between Niike and Wisor unfolds. Prince Silas is the first to react, drawing his pistol and, from across the room, firing at Niike. He only lands one shot, clipping his left shoulder, before he is shot through the head and instantly killed by General Ikano.

Shouting can be heard outside the room, with footsteps clearly approaching. Ikano is frozen; he's just murdered a prince in front of the rest of the royal family. The now-widowed Queen Lila and Niike's sister Kristi scream in horror at what is taking place in front of them.

Bang! Bang! Their screams are silenced permanently by Numenkor.

"What do we do?" Ikano asks in panic, looking around at the now-executed royal family while the footsteps get louder.

Numenkor does not hesitate. *Bang!* He puts a shot straight through the side of Ikano's head from nearly point-blank range.

The doors swing open, and the rest of the royal council and the king's guard enter the room.

"Don't shoot! There has been an attempted coup by General Ikano! We have several wounded royal family members!" Numenkor shouts.

The guards rush over to find four of the five already dead. Niike sits up, grasping his shoulder, his hands shaking.

What have I done? he thinks to himself as he looks around the room and sees the rest of his family lying in their own blood. Tears begin to well in his eyes.

"Niike needs medical attention immediately!" Numenkor says.

***

Eventually, after the royal doctor had removed the bullet fragments and closed the wound, Niike is brought upstairs to his bed.

"Secure the palace, and then inform the people what has happened. I will stay and protect our new king," Numenkor says.

With that, the doctor, the rest of the Knights, and the guards in Niike's room leave. Numenkor shuts the door behind them. The two are alone.

"I killed them. I killed them all with one shot," Niike says in shock, his body shaking.

"You did what you had to do for the good of the kingdom. You have saved us, King Niike. Because of your bravery, Ithora will survive."

"But at what cost? It wasn't supposed to be like this. Why couldn't he just do the right thing?"

"Do not blame yourself for your father's failings. He left you no choice."

Someone knocks on the door. Numenkor first grabs for his pistol, then relaxes and goes to reopen it. As soon as it's slightly cracked, Iawora bursts in. "Niike, I heard what happened, and I was so worried! Are you okay?"

Niike answers calmly in an attempt to assuage the frantic woman.

"Yes, I am going to be fine. It's great to see you, my love. I'm glad you're safe."

Iawora's response is simply to hug Niike as tightly as she can. Niike cringes in pain from his wound, yet he finally feels some calm. His remorse for his actions begins to fade as he realizes he has surely saved the most precious thing in his life.

Iawora continues. "Oh, Niike, I'm so sorry. What are you going to do?"

"Well, since my family's deaths have already been avenged, I will do the next best thing: rule in their honor and continue their mission to protect the Ithoran people." He turns to Numenkor.

"Send word to King Hylzar. I wish to address him at once in the throne room."

"Yes, my King." Numenkor nods with reassurance in his eyes.

***

When Dumelor arrives in the throne room, he finds it once again filled with dignitaries, as it was when he arrived. The difference this time is that Niike is sitting on the throne with Iawora beside him. He has donned bright yellow robes, while Iawora wears magenta, both taken directly from his parents' wardrobe and fitting loosely. The rest of Ithorans in the room opt for black. Niike keeps a straight face as Dumelor approaches the throne, but both he and Iawora are clearly weathered by the day's stress.

Once just a few feet away from the throne, Dumelor speaks softly. "King Niike, I'm so sorry for your loss. All of Valendor weeps for the Ithoran people tonight."

"Thank you for your kind words. You experienced similar tragedy yourself, so I know you can truly empathize with my sorrow. I am sorry if I appear unkempt, but I had to speak with you immediately."

"Your courage through this adversity is beyond admirable. You will make a strong leader for the Ithoran people."

"Let us all hope so." Niike looks around the room, then takes a deep breath and continues. "Moments before he was killed, my father informed my family, along with our highest-ranking Knight and general, of his decision to accept your offer of allegiance. It can only be concluded that the traitorous General Ikano was secretly working for the enemy, and wanted to stop such an action. I will not let my father's last wish be in vain. I will not let the Kingdom of Ithora fall to ruin under my rule. King Hylzar, as the new King of Ithora, I am accepting your offer of alliance."

3

Rise to Command

A group of soldiers, adorned in shimmering metal-plate armor and royal-blue capes with white embroidery, approaches Aurelia City from the north. They return from Ostis, an Aurelican military academy and city in the very north of their kingdom. Their travel on horseback has taken them far along the coastal Shoreline Road, weaving in-and-out of the Setara Mountains to finally reach the capital. They all live in the bustling city, but only one of them calls the royal palace their home.

Princess Skyler looks out across the Aurelian Bay at her hometown. With her helmet at her side, her long hair glistens in the day's early light and gently blows in the coastal wind. A morning fog covers the western shore and rolls into the bay, but nevertheless, the marble upper city shines a golden white as the sun beams down upon it from the east. The Elysian Gate Bridge, a single-sided drawbridge built to provide passage across the bay to and from the northern shore of the city, remains lowered. The southern marble tower that supports it reflects the sun like a beacon and stretches its cable-arms across the walkway.

Skyler and her companions ride across the bridge, pass through the marble Westfort castle, and move into the wooded lower city. Many Aurelicans step out from their houses to welcome the Princess's return with warm greetings, and Skyler waves back in response.

The third most-populous city in Amoria, Aurelia City is rarely rivaled in its beauty. It is built at the site of Ancient ruins on and around a range of hills on the north end of a peninsula. The peninsula shelters the Aurelian Bay, the location for the mouth of the Alcyon river, which links Panorus, Horven, and Aurelica together east-to-west all the way from the Shimmering Sea. Since its founding, Aurelia City has been the capital of Aurelica, and a place of wealth and power for all of Amoria.

The entire city is walled with marble. A twenty-five-foot wall wraps around the city's east and north coasts around a hundred feet from the shoreline, although city buildings do overflow the walls out to the bay's edge. In the west, a forty-five-foot wall rests against the ocean beach, with massive anti-naval cannons placed upon the wall's turrets. In the south lies what is simply known as the White Wall. Standing 400 feet high, with even taller turrets that slope outward near the ground, the White Wall was erected to ensure no southern invader, namely the Baylanders, could ever take the city by land. The White Wall is bookended by small fortresses to protect against any invaders who wish to circumnavigate it by bay or sea. These fortresses, along with the Westfort, connect all the walls together.

The lower city is full of wooden, mostly two-story rectangular buildings painted in what one might describe as neutral colors. The houses sometimes have bight colored trim or shutters, but maintain dark-colored pitched roofs. The buildings never run up against each other. Instead, they are interwoven within a forest of redwood trees, which rise 200 feet into the sky and go from being densely packed at the bottom of the city's hillslopes to scarcely dotted toward the lower city's top edge.

The upper city, on the other hand, creates quite the juxtaposition to its lower counterpart. Secluded by a fifty-foot wall of its own, the entire area is built of marble down to its very streets. Its buildings are lavish in their architecture, usually at least five stories tall, with unique designs, save for the commonality of their renowned towering marble columns.

Aurelica's land, while small in size, is the most fertile and provides the strongest minerals. Aurelia City epitomizes this wealth.

Skyler's group crosses under a gate in the upper wall and now rides on marble roads, weaving through heavy traffic of both people and horses making their way to and from their various appointments, errands, or work. They pass awe-inspiring buildings all the way to the palace, which is located atop the highest hill in the city.

The palace in itself is a sight to behold. Built around the contours of the high hill it rests upon, it is made up of three enormous buildings, all interconnected and arranged in the shape of a horseshoe facing southward. The buildings create a cove of a vast marble plaza, which is lined with statues and contains an extravagant thirty-foot-tall fountain in its center. The two outer buildings on the east and west sides of the palace are long three-story rectangles, overflowing onto their respective slopes, with columns lining their open faces in order to support their marble-tiled pitched roofs. The central building mirrors the architecture of its flankers, except for the fact that it towers twice as high while being one-third in length, contains both east and west wings to enjoin the other buildings, and has a 200-foot cylindrical spire at its northern end.

The soldiers dismount in front of the steps of the main building and bid farewell to Skyler. From there, she makes her way through a grand foyer up a wide royal-blue carpeted marble staircase leading to the throne room located on the building's north third floor. Pushing through fifteen-foot iron doors, she enters the rectangular room, which is supported by internal columns that rise all the way up to a high ceiling that doubles as the roof. The tallest windows in all of Amoria line the east and west walls, giving the throne room sweeping views of the city and natural light during the entirety of the day. The centerpiece of the room, besides the marble throne itself, is a long, decoratively-carved wooden table stretching from near the door up to the throne against the room's northern wall.

Upon entering, Skyler finds King Jackson Aurelia sitting at the edge of the table, dressed in the long white robes of Aurelican aristocrats. His are adorned with royal-blue accented cuffs, collar, and hemming, all with gold embroidery. He is an older man, but still looks fit to fight. Skyler likely has her own tall height to thank him for as well, as her stature even rivals her male compatriots in the army, while Jackson's own height places him above them. The King's entire table-space is covered in maps and other miscellaneous papers.

Jackson looks up from his work to greet her. "Sky!" he blurts happily. He grabs a scroll and rises from the throne. "I hear my daughter's return is a triumphant one."

Skyler proudly replies. "I passed all the tests, father, and have completed my training. I am officially an Aurelican Captain."

The two walk towards each other and embrace in the center of room. The morning sun shines brightly onto them through the east windows.

"Congratulations," he responds with sincerity. "Your mother and I had our doubts, but you have proved us wrong, and, in doing so, you have gained even more respect among Aurelicans... A shrewd political move as a member of the Aurelican royal family." He chuckles as he continues. "You will always be a favorite of the people."

"Thank you for your kind words, father, but I did not just complete this training as a formality. I did it so I could lead our people in battle."

Jackson's tone loses a bit of its excitement. "Ha. You may be qualified as a captain, but you must realize that you're one of the highest-ranking military officials in our army. You are a Princess. Why do we bestow this title, above your qualifications? Because your true role here is as a leader next to this throne. You have been groomed for it since you were a small child. Let our more hardened folk dream of glory in combat, for it is they who wish to ascend to the heights upon which you already stand."

"My place is beside our people on the battlefield."

"I admire your courage, although you may be a little too confident for my liking. Let us hope, in the unfortunate event you ever see the battlefield, that you have very good soldiers around you."

Skyler knows her father just wants to protect her, but she is annoyed that he believes she is not strong enough to defend herself. Before she can argue further, her father continues. "We will discuss this matter further later. In the meantime, I need to catch you up on recent developments in the south that are of concern. Queen Korza Amoria's forces have risen to the greatest heights this world has ever seen. The Baylander industrial machine is producing armor and weaponry at a blistering pace, and our spies report that military training exercises have doubled in the past few months. Our intelligence suggests an impending Baylander invasion of Zyber. The Baylanders seek to eliminate their threat in the south, as well as to claim their mines to support their economy, which, by the way, very much struggles to keep up with their overpopulation. Poverty and disease rise with no end in sight. The Baylander people are unsettled, and the Amorian family fears this. I have received word that Queen Korza herself traveled to Zyber to try to negotiate more friendly trade agreements, but the newly-crowned and tenacious Queen Zila Sumptet would not budge. While admirable, I fear the Zyberians are more vulnerable than they have been in centuries. They have an inexperienced Queen and a heavily outmatched army compared to their increasingly desperate neighbor. The balance of power in the world is shifting... and not in our favor."

Princess Skyler responds confidently. "The Baylanders would subjugate us all if they could. We must not abandon our ally. Send the fleet to their aid. They can be there in no time."

"Of course, I would in the event of an actual attack, but in this case, a show of force may only lead to heightened tensions between our own two kingdoms."

"Let there be tension. We can send our legions south through the Freelands and to the Baylander border. They will not dare attack anyone with their enemies surrounding them."

"Such an action would be a violation of the Treaty of Belfhen, thus technically mandating us to be an enemy of all other kingdoms, despite our long list of allies."

"You and I both know our allies are beholden to us. They would never stand against us. We cannot sit back while the Baylanders seek to establish the ways of the old world. The second we get complacent, Korza will move against us. Let me at least march our armies to the Baylander border south through Horven instead."

"We are not at war. Our armies will stay here," Jackson replies firmly. "And you would not be commanding them if we were. You are not qualified yet to lead such a force."

"Then let me set sail south with Admiral Tyler and the rest of the navy, at least to the southern Freelands border. We will call it a training exercise. That way, if the Baylanders try anything, our fleet will be able to move against them instantly."

"This, I do agree with, and I have already decided it will be our next move, although all the way down to the southern border is out of the question; I won't risk any incidents. Hopefully, it will temper Queen Korza's ambitions. You will not accompany the fleet, however. Leadership takes practice. You cannot command ships without any experience."

"How will I gain experience if you never let me go?"

"A fair question. I knew before you even returned you would want an assignment—your youthful ambition compels you. But I have a better opportunity for you; one with much lower risks and stakes. This will be a great chance for you to build a rapport with your troops and learn first-hand about the intricacies of command."

With this said, he hands over a scroll. Skyler unrolls the message and reads.

Dear King Jackson Aurelia,

It is with great reluctance that I compose this message.

I am invoking the agreed-upon Amoria Defense Accords that each kingdom be required to send reinforcements to maintain the garrison at the Eastfort.

I am aware that the fort has not asked for this garrison in fifty years. I would not do so unless I felt I had good reason to. On the day of my composition of this letter, a scouting party came back at half its original size, and with very unusual findings. To make matters worse, the surviving party members who returned to the fort have all died unexpectedly.

We believe that, when traveling farther east than ever before, it is highly likely our party encountered the savage Autoch. We are requesting a small force from each nation, only to assist in leading scouting parties to investigate the area and to search for our missing party members, along with providing defense of the fortress should an unlikely attack occur.

I reiterate that this request is a precautionary measure only, and that we have no official proof of Autoch involvement.

With regards,

Svender Ben

Svender Ben

Panorum Captain of the Eastfort

"You will take a cohort of the royal guard with you, will not ride out past the Panorum Gate, and will return immediately after the one-month garrison is completed," Jackson continues.

"If you're going to send me as far away from the action as possible, father, you can at least allow me to see the Eastern Expanse."

"You can see it from that watchtower. When you return, we can discuss a larger role for you if your appetite for soldiering isn't satiated yet. Do not discount the learning opportunity afforded to you. You ride first thing in the morning tomorrow."

"Thank you, father." Skyler gives a subtle bow and turns to exit.

Jackson looks on with wistful concern as she leaves. He can't help but think back to simpler times, when she was a young child full of innocence and devoid of the knowledge of the weight of the title bestowed upon her. Every day, the world inches towards turmoil, and he knows he won't be able to keep his daughter out of it forever.

After leaving the throne room, Skyler heads west to a balcony jutting from the side of the palace. She leans against the balustrade and peers out towards the ocean. However, disappointingly, she cannot see it, for the water and the entire lower city itself remain blanketed in a misty fog. Nevertheless, she looks on as if to wait hours for the fog to burn away, lost in her own thoughts.

4

PEACE OR GLORY

It is another quiet day in the Freelands. Morning has barely arrived, and a thick layer of fog flowing from the sea still rests snugly against the coastal hills. Blackbird chirps permeate the misty air above Baywood as, still amongst the clouds, Ariscles Shanis spars vigorously with his long-time friend Epicurus Mylor. The two young men are in their early twenties, and are of average height and fit build. Both had dreams dashed of being selected for the Inpyrium in the prior year, and are determined to earn acceptance into the most noble and elite academy in all of Amoria. For Ariscles and Epicurus especially, it is an opportunity to escape and see the whole world past the borders of the Freelands, an opportunity very rarely experienced and often eschewed by Freelanders—for why would one ever leave such a tranquil place?

Indeed, life in the Freelands is a peaceful one. The nation bears no army and no leaders; it is a pure democracy, with every citizen getting equal say and an equal vote in every discussion. The Treaty of Belfhen, signed by every kingdom around a hundred years ago to erect the Freelands as a compromise buffer zone between the New Baylands and Aurelica, shelters the nation from all external threats.

Each kingdom shares a responsibility to protect the sovereignty of the Freelands against any act of aggression.

The consistent peace has led to steady prosperity. Baywood has artfully-crafted two-story stone-and-wooden houses, along with profitable businesses scattered across its Cyprus-tree-dotted hillside. Each building is similar in size, but uniquely designed. It acts as an escape for many travelers from all over the world, who find serenity in its unburdened beauty. This has kept the tavern business booming in the town, to the benefit of Ariscles and Epicurus, who each work at the Westwood Inn, which is owned by Ariscles's family.

But business at the inn can wait. For now, they continue to spar. This is one of their best bouts, as neither can land a winning blow. At this point, they know each other's moves, and can practically foresee what the other will do next. They scramble across the hillside, over a fallen tree, and into the remaining stone foundations of an abandoned house. Both exhausted and frustrated, they use their off-hands to grab each other's sword-hands and try to muscle their wooden blades, despite the other's grip, into the other's chest. They seem to be at a standstill until, all of a sudden, Epicurus releases Ariscles's arm, ducks his off-balance strike, pulls his pistol, and fires a blank straight at Ariscles's chest.

The move and the sound itself catch Ariscles off guard. He stands still, contemplating whether he's just lost. "I guess that fraudulent move is what it takes to beat me, Epi," he says in jest.

"I am sure a Knight would have been ready for that one. Your enemy won't play by any sort of rules," Epi quips back.

"You both want to wake up the entire town!?" a voice interjects angrily. Ariscles's portly father, Rithus, comes lumbering up the hill, much to the chagrin of the two.

"What is it, father?" Ariscles asks, irritated.

"We are understaffed for breakfast today. We need you both down at the inn to help. The dining room is at full capacity, and your sister is at school."

"You know we use this time to train, father."

"You can find time to dream later, Aris. Now is the time to take care of your reality."

The reality is that the odds of being accepted to the Inpyrium are extremely low. Aris's great grandfather had made it, but none in his family had since him. It takes more than just effort, but natural gifts of intelligence, athleticism, and astuteness to be one of the few admitted—a level of natural ability that Aris and Epi simply did not have, no matter how hard they practiced—or so that's what they've been told.

Aris is not ready to accept his fate of being stuck in Baywood forever, but he is willing to accept his fate of having to go to work in the morning. He and Epi begrudgingly walk with Rithus back to the inn, which stands a few blocks uphill from the shore.

The Westwood Inn is massive by Freelands' standards. With over thirty rooms, and a restaurant taking up the entire bottom floor, the three-story wooden building with a pitched roof and an encircling porch is a landmark for the town. Travelers, however, come from places with much more spectacular buildings. The inn's real allure is its sweeping ocean views, its long-earned reputation for good food, and its diverse clientele.

In this case, guests are at the maximum from all corners of Amoria, identifiable by their attire. Those from Aurelica, the New Baylands, and Valendor generally wear tailcoats over waistcoats and collared button-down shirts along with trousers or breeches. Travelers from the Horventi Plain or Panorus dress in jeans and collared button-down shirts, while occasionally wearing broad brimmed hats with high crowns and vests. Freelander travelers conform to a mix of these styles. Meanwhile, to match their home climates, the northerners often wear fur caps, fur-lined frock coats, and wool trousers, while the southerners wear tunics or shorts and short-sleeve shirts. When in the most formal attire, women across all kingdoms, except for those in the far north and south, deviate from men by wearing high-waisted, slim, short-sleeve dresses with various accoutrements, especially shawls, while the men from the same regions generally conform to the fashion of Aurelica, the New Baylands, and Valendor.

As soon as they arrive, Aris and Epi immediately have to scramble to keep up with the heavy business, and to top it off, today, the patrons feel a little more manic and excited than usual. The two dash through the tables, each lit by an argand lamp, carrying food and drink to and from the bar. The guests are scarfing down their meals and leaving their seats quickly once finished. There's plenty of conversation, but it feels quiet for how many are dining.

After midday, Aris finally gets a chance to sit down and rest at the southwest corner table. The sun has not been able to break through the fog today, but it's now higher in the sky. He can see the ocean, and a dim white light shines through the room's windows, which surround the room in all direction except for in the north.

He picks the one seat at a table in the corner's shadow and begins to eat his own sandwich for lunch.

As quickly as the business came in, the business has left. The inn's restaurant is now near-empty. Epi walks over to his table and sits across from him.

"What a weird crowd today. It seemed like everyone was in a nervous hurry. The whole place felt... uneasy," Aris says in between bites, a little perplexed.

"That's because everyone was," Epi responds seriously. "Everyone is headed home."

"Why?"

"Tensions in the south are apparently rising. The whole region sounds like a bomb ready to explode."

"Korza would never move against her neighbors. It would be a diplomatic nightmare. It's all posturing," Aris says dismissively.

"The attempted coup in Ithora has destabilized the region. The far-southern nations are now both led by children, and Korza has an army even the Aurelicans in the north fear. If the Baylanders march south, no one will answer."

"The Baylanders rely on the northern kingdoms for trade. An unprovoked war against the Ithorans or the Zyberians would mean sanctions, and therefore starvation. Our patrons are simply spooked over political grandstanding."

Epi breaks his serious face and struggles to hide a grin. "Ah, come on. At least entertain the idea that there might be some excitement in your life-time. It's not the end of history." He reaches across the table and lightly slaps Aris on the arm.

This jovial jibe doesn't break Aris's mood. He sighs instead, glancing down towards the quiet Baywood streets nestled against the shore. "There may be some excitement in the far reaches of the world, but not here. Here, we are in the center of stability."

Epi smiles wider, as if Aris has said exactly what he wanted. "Then let us go to the far reaches."

"Ha! Don't be a fool. We have neither the time or money to do that, even if we wanted to."

"Don't be so certain... I overheard one of the tables saying that the Eastfort is calling for reinforcements. We can go out and see the expanse!"

Aris's dismissive disposition turns into curiosity. "Really? They haven't asked in our entire lifetime. What's the reason?"

"Some of their scouting party was lost or killed or something on their last trip. It's all very mysterious, but they think they could have been murdered by Autoch. Anyways, it's an all-expenses paid trip, we will meet people from all over Amoria, and maybe even get the chance to see real action for once—a can't-miss opportunity. We have to go."

"Oh, I don't know, Epi. Maybe there is something to this peace. This is a good life we have here, and we're going to risk it to go fight in the far reaches of the world? While I admire your ambitious courage, I cannot muster the same. Besides, who would work in our stead at the inn?"

"Oh, please. Your parents can hire a couple extra hands for a few weeks. Think about it—I heard the valley train comes into the station the day after tomorrow to pick up volunteers. We can take a wagon over there first thing in the morning. It will only be around a month, and there is little chance we actually see combat. The Autoch haven't been seen for countless years anyways. Besides, I'm going, and I think you're going to be pretty jealous of all my stories when I come back."

"Be honest—you only want me to go so I can protect you. You can't survive without me," Aris says laughingly.

"Well then, I guess you will feel pretty responsible if I don't make it back." Epi follows with a wink while getting up and leaving to pack, abandoning Aris to self-contemplation.

***

Aris struggles to focus during his night shift, for the decision weighs heavily on his mind. He finishes up his work, then walks out to the back porch of the inn. Most guests have gone to bed. The air is quiet save for the sound of low waves crashing on the shore. Aris stares into the night horizon with the light of the inn illuminating his back and the light of the stars reflecting off the seemingly infinite ocean.

Out of nowhere, he has been presented what seems like a life-changing opportunity in a life with zero opportunities. Deep down, after his rejection from the Inpyrium, he has been resigned to his fate. He has accepted the normality of the Freelands, but this normalcy, however peaceful, still drowns his spirit. He can feel himself meandering aimlessly through life as it passes him by.

After considerable time, Aris breaks his frozen stance and walks around the now-calm Westwood Inn. He's on his way to pack, for, above all things, his heart overcomes his head. He desires an opportunity at a life of grandeur, rather than one of naïve serenity.

5

The Board is Set

A steady rain crashes onto Ithor's Gift. The streaming water and clouds block out the rising moon and stars.

"The night will be dark. The conditions are perfect," Niike states as he stands drenched, looking out over the water. He speaks with more confidence than ever before, now that he has gotten used to the title of King preceding his name.

Dumelor, standing a few feet behind and underneath the awning of a Vethoran market, replies. "My soldiers are in position. Now is the time to strike."

Over a thousand wooden rowboats, large enough to fit ten to fifteen Ithorans, embarked from Okondo earlier in the week, and now lie dormant at the docks along the lakeshore.

"We will move at once. Tell your soldiers to do the same," Niike says back to Dumelor.

"Events are in motion that will reshape our world. My army landed unseen yesterday, and are already securing the border in secret, as planned. Now, it is your time to secure your people's future." With that, Dumelor steps back into the shadow and disappears.

Niike had seen some Valendi soldiers amassing in town the day before, but he had not even seen them set off. *In secret indeed,* he thinks to himself; impressed already with Dumelor's execution. He turns and walks over to the makeshift command hut, which is stilted, like all of the Ithoran buildings along the lake.

"Rally your legions. The invasion commences at once," he orders.

The Ithoran generals, including Niike's newly appointed commander, Sir Numenkor, have to hide their apprehension. The war is upon them, and death and destruction are bound to follow. They disperse quickly.

Niike walks to his quarters in the back of the hut. There, Iawora lays in their bed, restless, with worried eyes. "I fear you sail to never return," she musters the strength to say.

"There will be risk and there will be danger, but the war will be over before you know it. We will move like a viper through the sands of Zyber and strike down the capital before the little girl Zila can even react. Besides, no army will stand between me and returning to you. Our destiny lies together, in a world where finally we can be at peace, unquestioned and unapologetic in our love."

Iawora is not quite persuaded by his words. "Niike, where are the Valendi forces? They should be with you. What if Dumelor is really who your father initially thought he was? It would be our end."

"My father was complacent, and paid for it with his life. Dumelor is a great man, and the Valendi will not let us down. Tonight, I set sail for him, for you, and for all our people—to reclaim our destiny."

Numenkor enters the room. "My King, the troops have begun to board the ships. It is time for you to put on your armor and take command."

"Thank you, Commander Baw."

Numenkor exits. Niike turns to follow, then stops, turns back, and gives Iawora a long kiss. She wraps her arms around him so as to not let him leave. Her eyes water.

Niike gives his last assurance. "Fear is for those who know deep down that defeat is their fate. I have no fear. I will see you soon."

***

A short time later, Niike exits the armory adorned in his royal plates. The traditional Ithoran armor is comprised of a thin iron chest plate, helmet, shoulder, and shin guards. Underneath, they wear brown, also thin, cloth shirts and shorts, which have no sleeves and are short on the thighs respectively. Their wrist and thigh guards, along with their shoes, are made of leather. The officers' plate armor is painted vibrant colors by each individual wearer. Niike has painted his helmet with three bright lime-green stripes on its left side, and has painted his shoulder and chest plates with three light-blue stripes on their front and back right. The final touches to his outfit are his weapons—a seven-shot revolver with a wood finish and a standard Ithoran curved sword with a golden ornamental hilt fit for a king.

With the rain still steadily falling, he steps onto his boat. He nods across the water to the boat next to him, and an Ithoran soldier grabs a large, curved wooden horn and lets loose a deep and deafening sound that cuts through rain.

The Ithorans begin to row.

The boats glide across the lake, its glassy surface only disturbed by rippling raindrops. The comforting humidity of the Ithoran Jungle slowly leaves them, and the cool, empty air of the desert night greets them. It takes some time to cross the distance between Vethoran and the Zyberian city of Inwutet, and Niike keeps the pace slow so that he will not overtire his army before battle.

Finally, he can make out Fort Tite, which rests on an isthmus in the center of the city's wide bay. Inwutet and its impressive fortress is built with traditional light-brown Zyberian sandstone. The city has a small wall encircling it except for where it borders the lake. Fort Tite, however, has imposing seventy-five-foot walls surrounding it in the shape of a diamond, with the largest cannons Niike has ever seen resting on the three turret-corners adjacent to the lake. Those cannons wouldn't be too much use against the Ithorans' smaller boats, but they have yet to fire, anyways, despite the fact that the Ithorans are definitely in their range.

The plan is working. They have not been seen.

As they approach closer and closer, Niike braces with anticipation of cannon-fire, but it does not come; his forces reach the isthmus untouched. One by one, their boats wash ashore on the gently sloped beach, and the Ithorans flood the little space they can occupy before the fort walls.

Each boat carries a portion of a ladder. The parts are carried to the walls, where they can be combined. Once pieced-together, the ladders are raised against the wall, and the Ithorans begin to climb.

Still, there is no sign of a defense.

The first Ithorans reach the top and quickly head to each of the four turrets. There, they find the cannons unmanned. Each turret has closed hatches where troops can move up through to its ramparts or down through to the fortress floor. Ithoran soldiers rip open the top hatch on the front turret facing the lake to find twelve Zyberian soldiers, still in their armor, stirring from a drunken slumber.

Zyberians wear iron metal armor, painted white to deflect the sun, with white tunics and capes with gold embroidery. The soldiers are more interested in using their capes as blankets than decoration in this case. They had sheltered from the night's rain, figuring no boat would dare travel in the weather, nor giving any thought to the idea of an enemy invasion.

They were wrong, and they now pay for it. Before any of them can muster a shout, the Ithoran soldiers fall upon them. Swords plunge straight into their hearts and cut their throats. The walls are already taken, and hundreds of Ithorans are moving towards the fortress floor.

All this marching cannot go unnoticed forever, though. From the inner keep, one of the rare guards on duty who is still doing his job spots the soldiers scrambling upon the walls. He immediately runs to the alarm bell and begins ringing it. He manages to get four solid rings off before Niike, who has now summited the wall as well, orders him shot down. Over a hundred soldiers fire their rifles at the bell tower at the same time, blasting the guard off as if he'd been hit by hurricane winds. He has done enough, however; the fortress is awake and alert.

Zyberian soldiers quickly lock and brace the gate of the inner keep as Ithorans flood the fort's courtyard from the turrets. The

Ithorans have not brought any siege tools to break through, but it is no matter. Niike orders the black-powder for the cannons to be taken from the walls and brought to rest against the keep door. There are a few moments of silent tension, but once the powder is in place, it takes just a smattering of shots from a safe distance to ignite the makeshift bomb and blast the doors inward, killing more Zyberian soldiers in the process.

The first wave of Ithorans to enter the keep are met with a volley of rifle fire, as are the second, and the third, and the fourth… yet they just keep coming. The Zyberians simply do not have enough ammo to hold off their enemy.

As the Ithoran soldiers finally reach the outnumbered Zyberians inside and engage them in hand-to-hand combat, Niike charges in. The slaughter has begun.

The forces in the main hall are overwhelmed, including the fortress's captain. Once they are mercilessly dealt with, the Ithoran forces push into every hallway and room. No Zyberian stationed in the fort survives.

***

The rain slows, and the clouds are clearing. Niike walks out of the fortress gate to gaze upon Inwutet. A red sunrise lights the sandstone buildings, and the clay mountains behind them aglow, along with the numerous Ithoran boats at the shore.

Numenkor walks up from the city to Niike, and the two head back toward it together. "The city has surrendered. There was no fighting," Numenkor reports.

"A flawless victory," Niike boasts. "This will be even easier than I imagined."

"It's still a long road to the capital, and Dumelor needs to do his part."

"His line will hold," Niike says confidently. "The kingdom of Ithora is finally strong in the face of its enemies."

"What of the townspeople, sir? We cannot afford to carry prisoners around the Senduine."

"No, we cannot, nor can we spare troops to govern them. Have them all taken as slaves and delivered back to Ithora as a gift from their triumphant King."

"That may be unpopular amongst the other kingdoms. Slavery is not as widespread as it once was."

"Maybe so, but I am sure they would prefer it to the alternative. Besides, Zyber must pay for their treachery. Much Ithoran blood will spilled at the cost of Zyberian greed."

"I will see it done."

Now at the outskirts of Inwutet, Numenkor carries on back to the town center. Niike pauses to bask in his victory for a few more moments when Dumelor appears, walking over to him from the north. He greets Niike with a smile. "I am not sure any King has had such a successful first battle."

Niike is admittedly perplexed about how Dumelor has gotten there, but his relief and excitement from his first victory easily assuages his curiosity. "Hopefully, there are many more victories to come," he replies.

"Korza will not be happy about this one, but don't worry, my soldiers will hold her. Keep your focus on reaching the coast."

"You have such confidence in your army going against the strongest military in the world."

"The key is that we won't be. I know Korza all too well. The paranoid Queen will not divert her entire army to fight for a foreign kingdom. She distrusts the northerners, especially her greatest rival and threat, the Aurelicans. Your force will never see combat with the Baylanders."

"I will hold you to that."

"I haven't let you down yet, have I?" Dumelor turns and walks back up the beach north, where Niike can make out his horse in the distance.

Niike looks away and moves to join Numenkor in evaluating his first victory's bounty.

6

An Eastern Escape

It has been a long march from the last Alcyon Railroad stop in Starlinden, but Aris and Epi don't mind. Both of them had never even seen the Orus mountains, much less hiked across them; the trip has given them newfound excitement and energy with every step they take further.

Aris already believes he has made the right choice. *What an experience this has been*, he thinks as he stares in awe at nature's surroundings. *And what an experience it will be.*

Heavily pine forested slopes have given way to rockier, sparsely vegetated mountains as they neared their destination. Spring snow still appears in shaded patches and caps the mountaintops, while the thin air around them remains chilled. A harsh wind whips through the Orus Pass, and high clouds dot half of the sky.

The Eastfort comes into view around midday, and they see something much different than had been the case for many years—the fort is actually fully occupied. Thousands now stand where only a couple hundred are usually garrisoned. Much of the new force is made up of Panorum soldiers who have made the short trip to set an example and provide a baseline garrison for the fort.

Still, there are other major delegations. Horven and Ordenwood have both sent large contingents, along with key personnel, in an effort to garner political favor with Panorus, as the kingdom is Amoria's largest supplier of stone and precious metals. Horven hardly produces any stone of its own, and Ordenwood's mountainous stone region lies too far north to be inhabitable for most of the year.

Jynland brought only volunteers to the Eastfort. The sparsely populated northern kingdom generally cares little for worldly affairs. Outsiders rarely travel there, and the Jyn people almost never have to concern themselves with the conflicts of the south, given the fact that they are so isolated. Jynland is also going through its own problems right now. A natural disaster has uprooted many of its most northern inhabitants and has greatly impacted its fur industry. The kingdom has little attention to spare on southern adventures.

Aurelica's delegation is small as well, for their concern with southern geopolitical instability has required them to leave their real soldiers at home. But the prudent King Jackson has sent some of his finest guards, along with his daughter, as a sign of goodwill.

That goodwill could not be afforded by those actually now at war in the south. None of the southern kingdoms have sent any aid, technically in violation of the Amoria Defense Accords. King Thandus Vodner of Panorus has already officially forgiven them for their absence, however, given their circumstances and the fact that he isn't convinced of the necessity of the call to arms in the first place.

Aris and Epi, along with the rest of the Freelander volunteers, are the final group to arrive at the Eastfort. While Aris has seen travelers from these kingdoms before, it is hard not to be excited to see all the soldiers together in one place and to feel like he is part of it.

He passes through the fort, moving through each force, all with similar yet distinctive vesture. In Amoria, armor can be made of many different materials and colors, but generally covers several key areas with similar parts; a standard armor set is made of metal and consists of shin-guards, thigh-guards, bracers, some form of a chest-plate, shoulder-plates, and a helmet. This leaves some body parts more exposed in exchange for mobility. Other kingdoms eschew plate armor for more nimble chainmail dress, which generally drapes from over the shoulders down to above the knees.

Indeed, the Panorum soldiers wear hooded chainmail with dark-green or white cloaks over the top, depending on the season. Underneath, they wear long-sleeve shirts and breeches made of wool along with tall boots. Most of the Panorum soldiers are wearing their green attire, as the snows have already melted below the Orus peaks.

The Horven soldiers are wearing bronze plate armor head-to-toe, with light-golden-brown shirts and breeches made of cotton underneath. Their helmets have cheek-guards and provide shielding for the back of their necks, but lack full face-guards. Leather boots that extend to the mid-calf with pointed toes and small heels are standard issue for their army as well.

The Ordish are dressed for colder weather. They wear wool trousers and long-sleeve shirts with leather shoulder pads, bracers and shin guards, fur caps, and chainmail dress covering their chest and thighs. They also often wear fur-lined hooded frock coats, which are multicolored brown to help camouflage them in the arbor environments of their kingdom. Unlike other soldiers, their primary weapons are axes rather than swords, due to their multi-use purpose in their forested home of Ordenwood.

The Jyn are in heavy winter attire, which is no surprise given their frigid homeland. It consists of helmetless iron plate armor set lined with fur, with wool pants and long-sleeve shirts underneath, all topped off with hooded fur cloaks draped around them.

Lastly, the Aurelicans don their traditional full steel plate armor, rounded off by royal-blue capes with white embroidery. Their helmets cover their entire heads save for their ears, and the area of their face is exposed by T-shaped slits cut in their visors. They wear white cotton breeches, socks of varying length, and shirts underneath with brogans for shoes. Some sport royal-blue long-coats with gold buttons and white hemming and embroidery over their armor to keep warm. Ranking Aurelican officers have special-colored bracers, with captains and above wearing white-painted versions.

Aris and Epi are guided by a Panorum colonel to hollow stone buildings that will act as their homes for the month. They are sharing it with several other Panorum soldiers, as the mercenary Freelanders are to be spread out throughout the makeshift army. To their delight, Aris and Epi still get to remain in the same company, however, despite being assigned to different barracks.

The affable-looking Captain Sendis greets them just outside of their new abodes. "Gentlemen, we are happy to have you two join us for this little escapade. I have word from Captain Ben that we will be embarking on our scouting mission in two weeks. Until then, sharpen your soldiering skills with our forces here, and enjoy the company of the Eastfort. This should be a fun month."

Sendis, along with the rest of the company made up of Panorum men and women in their twenties and early thirties, seems to be in a very good mood. It is as if this trip to the Eastfort is one big paid vacation for the soldiers, just as Epi said. For them, it's an escape from the dullness of wherever they've been stationed throughout the endless Orus range.

Sendis's mood has an alleviating effect on Aris, who now feels like he isn't really in any danger at all. He's on vacation with the soldiers too.

***

That night, with all the various forces now settled in, Captain Svender Ben calls a meeting of the key leaders of each group in the main hall of the keep. As the Jyn and Freelanders did not bring any high-ranking leaders, they do not have any representatives. That leaves three people to attend, along with the two Knights sent from the Inpyrium. Princess Skyler attends for the Aurelicans, Commander Ny Azen attends for the Horventi, and Captain Orvden Liber represents Ordenwood.

Azen is the top general of the Horventi Army, and brings a strong veteran leadership presence to the group. Although only in his late thirties, he has commanded the Horventi army for nine years now. Born into one of Horven's wealthiest farming families, the handsome Azen is known by all Horventi for his strength, athleticism, and skill with a blade. This is perhaps why he quickly caught the eye of the Horventi King Venden Farrow as the top soldier in his personal guard. By taking him on as his protégé, Venden quickly fast-tracked Azen through the Horventi ranks. Though he lacks real battle experience, his soldiers' reverence for him seems limitless.

Liber, nicknamed the Northern Falcon, is an Ordish Captain who is world-renowned for his sharpshooting ability and axe-handling. It is said he once shot five men before any could draw their pistol, and that he holds the record for the furthest kill in history, when he shot a man from atop a tree allegedly a mile away. The tales of the raccoon-fur-capped Liber and his sharpshooter squadron's adventures in Ordenwood captivate audiences across all of the kingdoms, and have turned him into a celebrity everywhere he travels. This leads most to be surprised when they meet him and find that he is of short stature with an affable personality. It can be deceiving, however, for to his enemies he is equally minacious.

The two Knights in attendance are Gonder Quijyn and Jet Ikonobo. Sir Gonder is an old and tall man from Jynland who is one of the most respected Inpyrian Knights. He maintains a position as a historian and professor at the Inpyrium, where he has garnered a reputation as a caring mentor and wise friend. Due to his extensive and tireless research, his knowledge of the Ancients is rivaled only by the Inpyrian Lords themselves, and maybe his former pupil at the academy, Sir Hylzar Dumelor.

Sir Jet is a younger man from Ithora who is one of Gonder's top scholars. Gonder chose him to accompany him on this quest for two reasons: he performs well in his classes, and is the one of the best young swordsmen in the Inpyrium Academy. Gonder reasons the latter will be important if there truly is an Autoch threat on their eastern trip. Jet himself is not happy to be brought on this "boring" trip, however. He is only here because the respected Gonder insisted. He would much rather be continuing his training at the Inpyrium, as his desire to improve his combat skills outweighs his interest in scholarly pursuits.

The two wear traditional Inpyrian clothes, which entails jersey-fabric, hooded, button-down long-coats and tunics underneath reinforced leather armor sets. All of their armor is worn beneath their long-coats except for their shoulder pauldrons. Gonder's clothing and armor is brown, and his tunic is lighter in color, while Jet wears a similar tunic and armor, but sports a black long-coat and has dark red stripes painted on his left pauldron. Their armor is extremely valuable, as it is as light as leather, but as strong as steel. Each Inpyrian crafts their own armor as a part of their training, infusing the leather with crystal flakes to give it its strength. The process is impossible without a deep connection with the natural energy of the world. Fostering this connection is believed to be the most important skill learned at the Inpyrium.

Once all have arrived and settled in, Captain Ben begins the meeting. "Thank you all for showing your support here today. I imagine my letter looked strange, but I had to act on what happened here in this very room."

He gives a subtle glance to the place on the floor where Tharmir and Sedgen perished. The stains of their blood faintly remain.

"The tales of what occurred here are disturbing," Gonder remarks. "I can only imagine what it was like to have seen it in person."

"My goal for this increased garrison is, first and foremost, to secure the Panorum Gate, but I feel equally obliged to discover what really happened to my scouting party. There is even a chance some still live and need our help."

"We much desire to learn the truth as well, Captain Ben," Azen interjects.

"If there truly is an Autoch threat, I will take my squadron out into the expanse and personally exact retribution for your fallen kin, Captain," Orvden adds confidently in his rugged drawl Ordish accent.

"I appreciate your sentiment, but you will not need to go alone. That's why we have all the soldiers here. The plan is to conduct preliminary scouting trips into the expanse to ensure a clear route to the forest where Tharmir's scouting party ran into trouble. Then, I will personally lead a sizable force to explore the forest," Ben replies.

"I would tread carefully here," Gonder cautions. "Something feels off about this whole thing. The physical disruption can be felt in this very room. Ben, you should bring Jet and me with you to this forest you speak of."

"It is a long journey, but I of course welcome any Knight presence. Does anyone have any issues with the plan? Princess Skyler?"

The others nod in agreement with Ben as Skyler begins her answer. "The Aurelicans will do their duty here, but we will not be joining the final trip east without physical evidence of an Autoch threat. Our place lies with our interests in the south. We must return as soon as we can to ensure stability in the region."

"Ha! The majority of your force stays at home anyways. Are you afraid, young Skyler?" Orvden quips.

Skyler jabs back. "We need all of our attention focused on our tangible threats. Not tall tales far away from our home."

She learned of the Ithoran invasion on her way out to the Eastfort, and she is frustrated that she is away from the action in the south—her perceived real chance to shine as a new captain in the army. She is not going to stay in the Orus Mountains any longer than she needs to.

Ben continues. "Understood, Skyler. Let us hope we find nothing. That is all I had for this brief meeting. Feel free to reach out to me personally at any time if you need something."

The group disperses, with Skyler storming out, annoyed at her situation, to the amusement of Captain Liber, who exits slowly, chatting with Commander Azen. Ben retreats to study papers at his desk.

Jet moves to leave, but Gonder hesitates for a moment and strokes his chin, causing Jet to stop and wait up for him. Finally, Gonder turns and heads for the doors. He and Jet walk out onto the fortress steps toward their temporary home in the inner fort. Jet can clearly notice Gonder is troubled. "Sir Gonder, what did you feel in there?"

"Something I have never felt before, which makes me feel uneasy about this whole thing. It didn't feel like the Autoch. It felt like something more distant... elusive."

"'Elusive?' The power to elude the senses of an Inpyrian Knight is known only by the strongest Inpyrians themselves."

"Indeed. Something is out of place, and I am missing it. Contrary to the conclave's opinion, our presence here was definitely warranted and needed. Stay keen. We have much work to do."

7

History Returns

This place is unknown. It lies in an old and thick jungle that, with time, has become overgrown.

The buildings are ancient and massive, built of gray sandstone turned dark by ash. The unusual architecture is not of the people of Amoria; it predates them. It does have some consistency, however. Each structure has a main building in its center surrounded by a rectangular enclosure with a courtyard in the empty space. The walls defining the enclosures are lined by galleries with colonettes supporting their pitched roofs. Four one-to-two story buildings are built into each enclosure structure, one on each side. Long, raised stone passageways lead to each structure's front and only entrance. Rigid spires rise from both the central buildings and the outer enclosures. When one is close enough, it's possible to make out ancient drawings and illegible writings carved into almost every sandstone brick.

Hylzar Dumelor rides through the overgrown city-ruins and arrives at a twenty-foot-tall entranceway towards its southeastern end. The wooden doors of this enclosure lay open, rotting away and barely hanging to their hinges. He dismounts and walks through the structure's courtyard to the main building.

This building is more impressive than the rest in the city in both size and profoundness. It rests upon a three-tiered pyramid with steep stairs leading up to its entrance. The building itself is wider than it is long, with six spires paired across with each other on every corner and in the building's center. Colonettes spaced three inches from each other support the pitched roof and replace what would be a wall on all sides. The towering entryway rises all the way to the roof and cuts directly through the front spire. There is no door.

Dumelor walks right in.

The long and dark room he enters is only lit by the natural light coming from the entryway and the slits in the column wall. It has a grand obsidian table covered in maps and writings stretching from the left end of the room all the way to the right. Directly across from the entrance is an extravagant obsidian chair with a six-pronged crystal glowing black set in its top. All of the interior furniture, pillars, and walls are engraved with markings from some foreign language.

"I foresaw you coming," a voice says from the shadow. "What news from the west?"

A hooded woman steps forward, clutching an ancient sword in her right hand to use as a cane. The sword is a sight in itself, as it has an expertly detailed shimmering-yet-black obsidian pommel and an enlarged asymmetrical triangular blade-tip. The woman looks as if she is beyond a hundred years old and wears ragged black-silk robes of the Valendi over brown leather armor. Her robes' cuffs and collars are embroidered with intricate white-silk designs. She gingerly walks towards the chair while Hylzar responds.

"The Ithorans have joined us and invaded Zyber. As anticipated, the Prince was vulnerable, and has sided with our cause. In accordance with their pact, the Baylanders moved the majority of their army south and sought to crush the invaders. What they were not ready for was our ambush in the Zyberian Highlands. Valendi strike-forces dressed as Ithorans attacked the Baylanders at key chokepoints and forced them to retreat and regroup. Our plan has worked to perfection. Now, I believe it is time to commence the second phase. I have given orders to Xastix to begin our full-scale invasion."

"Good." The hooded woman grabs the crystal from the chair and sets it into an open space in her sword hilt at the intersection of the guard and the blade. She pushes herself upright with the makeshift cane and morphs right before Hylzar's eyes. Her skin tightens; her posture straightens; her muscles tone. Within moments, she has the appearance of a beautiful and healthy woman no older than thirty-five. Every one of her physical features are near immaculate. Dumelor is unsurprised.

"I see you still do not fear an eruption," he says, smiling.

"They come from time to time, but are always small and insignificant. If the mountain decides to strike me down now, then so be it. I have lived long enough to know that it won't." The woman's younger voice is soft yet forceful.

She walks, now unaided, over to her maps on the obsidian table. "The people of Amoria are already on their back foot. Once the New Baylands flips to our side, there will be no stopping us."

She pauses, then continues. "Now, I have other news to report."

Hylzar gives a look of slight puzzlement.

"This city was discovered not long ago by a Panorum scouting party."

"I saw the message. It's nothing," Hylzar says dismissively. "No one survived, and the fortress captain doesn't understand what happened."

"He may not understand now, but he will seek to. He will surely send a more formidable force to investigate. Already, our element of surprise has been weakened." Gesturing to the Orus Pass on her map, she continues. "The Eastfort will stand properly garrisoned. We cannot afford the chance to be discovered. It would foil everything we've planned, everything I have worked for, for all of these years..."

The woman stares into the void for a moment before refocusing. "Izedar and the rest of the other acolytes have completed their training and have been given command of the Autoch. By manipulating the Diluvion Crystal, I can cover their advance to Starlinden, but no further, for the farther it reaches, the more difficult it is to bend it to my will. As we speak, the Autoch march to their target."

"Are you sure you can control that crystal's power?" Dumelor says worriedly. "I have seen the results of its wroth first-hand."

"I have spent more years studying it than you have lived. I assure you, Izedar will be quite safe."

Dumelor grunts while pondering his next words. He cannot hide his apprehension. "Nevertheless, it is too soon. Zyber must fall first. Our armies will be stretched too thin."

"We do not have a choice. We must accelerate our pace. The Valendi and Ithorans will keep their focus south. Once the New Baylands and Zyber are under our control, your forces will join the Autoch in the north."

"We will need every sword and rifle we can get to take Aurelia City, and my effort to retrieve the other crystal at Castle Karvus has only just begun. I believe we must have it to keep the conquered kingdoms in line and, more importantly, to ensure it's not used against us."

"They know not of it. I assure you, our unprecedented armies will keep them in line. There will be enough swords as long as we stand by our strategy and Xastix and Izedar can execute their parts. Besides, the mishap with the Panorum scouting party may work to our advantage. My spies tell me several key foreign dignitaries—including a princess of Aurelica, the head Horventi commander, and the brutish Captain Liber—all plan to participate in the garrison. Izedar now has the opportunity to deliver a crippling blow across all of Amoria with his very first strike. I have given him specific orders to eliminate all high-value targets garrisoned there."

"He will not let us down," Dumelor assures her before changing the subject. "And what of my crystal?"

"I have it here. It is ready at last, and its first test subject appears to have been a resounding success. The key final process is the blood. Once his blood is infused, he will be able to control it, but be careful—if the blood is ever cross-contaminated, it will wipe out the original controller's power." The hooded woman extends her arm and drops a glowing five-sided dark-red crystal with a large crack across it into Dumelor's hand. "I hope you are right about her."

"I know her all too well. She just needs a bit of forceful persuasion to unlock her repressed ambition."

"Very well. Go now. Do what must be done and secure Amoria for Valendor. Soon, we shall return to our prominence, and those who betrayed us shall finally meet their rightful judgement."

Hylzar looks into the women's eyes for a moment while clutching the crystal firmly in his grip then turns and hurriedly exits. The skip in the timeline has unsettled him. To rush their plan puts pressure on him and all of his forces.

There can be no mistakes.

8

Valendor's Deception

General Ryder Medinus rides north along the shore of the Olovor Bay on an overcast day. A handsome man in his late thirties, and the highest-ranking officer in the Baylander army, he wears brown leather boots, white cloth breeches, a white long-sleeve shirt, and a formal Baylander red cape. His disposition radiates confidence and ambition, which has helped him climb to his top rank despite his plebeian background. He keeps a hurried speed, for he has been summoned to Queen Korza's throne room.

The throne room is in the center of the royal palace, which also sits exactly in the center of Ezebandia, the capital of the New Baylands. The palace consists of five ten-story buildings arranged in a pentagon formation, surrounded by a forty-foot bastion-style fort wall which connects to the buildings' outer faces at their fifth floor. An additional building that doubles as a train station juts from the point of the pentagon to its center. Each building in the palace is built of beautiful red-and-orange brick with white wooden window facades and steep, slate-tiled, black roofs. The palace grounds are adorned with green grass and oak trees. The palace sticks out in the bustling city of Ezebandia, as most buildings are built out of brick and pressed tightly together, with little space for any vegetation.

Ezebandia sits on the western coast of the New Baylands, nestled between the ocean shore and the Rolling Hills. It is the largest and most populous city in Amoria by far, giving it bustling streets, turbulent markets, factories with towering smokestacks, and massive dockyards along Olovor Bay.

Ryder weaves his way on horseback through the city's southwest gate and onto dirt roads. Pressed for time, he dodges carriages and foot-traffic, causing quite a ruckus amongst the crowds. With the whole city built on flat land, and every street tightly squeezed by roughly five-story townhouses, it's fairly easy to get lost. Ryder, however, has an easier time due to his destination. He finds one of the six main cobblestone avenues in the city and rides northeast. Each major avenue leads diagonally to-and-from a circular road in the center of the city. The road encircles the palace.

After his short escapade through Ezebandia, Ryder arrives at the palace gate. The golden-tipped iron gate built into the front building swings open in anticipation of his arrival. Ryder dismounts his horse and steps through into the palace where he is greeted by the captain of the royal guard, Jof Dunharrow.

"General Medinus, welcome-back to Ezebandia. It is always a pleasure to see you in these halls."

"A pleasure to see you as well, Captain Dunharrow. When I have more time, I would like to catch up and grab dinner, like the old days down at The Ocean Grove."

"I am afraid your time is going to be hard to find for many days, Ryder. There is ill news in the east. The Queen wishes to speak with you at once."

"I shouldn't keep her waiting, then."

The two walk through the front structure and out its back towards the main building in the center of the palace.

Jof is an old man who once was the commanding general of the army himself. Though his age has slowed his physical ability, he remains a skilled warrior and a valued advisor to the Queen. He and Ryder met long ago at the Baylander officer academy at Coyote Cape. Since then, the two have always kept a close relationship, with Jof often giving Ryder wise council as he racked up promotions. Since Jof is on-duty, he wears typical Baylander full steel plate armor, complete with a red cape and two red stripes on his shoulder plates, signifying his rank. He carries his standard-issue helmet at his side, which has a single slit for the eyes and a retractable vented visor, and his royal guard-issue long rifle with a detachable scope and bayonet on his back.

The two eventually enter the throne room on the top floor. Its wooden interior is flanked by brick columns and brightened by natural light beaming in from several skylights in the ceiling. Beautiful paintings depicting historical events of the old world and the new grace the walls, with lamps in between each. A red carpet lined with gold embroidery leads from the entrance to the throne itself on the room's left, which is made of gold and cushioned with red-velvet.

There, Queen Korza Amoria sits alone, draped in red, white, and gold robes over a hardly-visible white dress. In her left hand, she grasps a silver scepter that has a single gold-glowing crystal set near its top, and she wears a golden crown that seems to have its own space for a crystal at its center. The Queen is older, but her beauty and power are both still undeniable. She sits tall on her throne and sports elegantly-curled hair draping past her shoulders. Her mere presence inspires fear, loyalty, revere, and awe from her people, for the Amoria family are the last known descendants of the old world's royalty. She represents the persistence of the New Baylands' glorified history, a deitylike figure in the eyes of many.

"My Queen, it is an honor, as always." Ryder bows as he arrives before her, while Jof tails him, offset a few feet behind. "I came as soon as I heard you sent for me. I will make haste back to the battlefield once your message is delivered. We have been delayed at the Zyberian border, and must intercept the sweeping Ithoran army before they reach the coast."

The Queen is stoic, and answers Ryder as if he has not spoken. "The world is upside down, General Medinus." Korza speaks with a measured and powerful tempo. "You are to withdraw all of our troops who are not necessary to secure the border."

"But my Queen, the pact..."

"We have sworn to protect others, but who will defend us in these trying times? An unspoken alliance as old as the beginning of Amoria, forsaken. My ancestors... Our people, who died defending the Valendi in the old world, recoil in their graves."

"I don't understand..."

"It was a diversion, a calculation, a trap... and I fell for it. The Ithorans were the bait. The real prize was our cities and fortifications, undefended in the east." She pauses to collect her words, then continues. "Our spies reveal the treacherous Hylzar Dumelor has sent out the entire Valendi army from Dor-Eletor. They will reach our major cities of Bandine and Philippia before our army can recover. I have sent word for an immediate evacuation, but it will be slow and cumbersome. We cannot move the people and supplies quickly enough."

"What would you have me do?" Ryder feels a rare anxiety. The war in the south is low-stakes; a great opportunity for him to showcase his prowess and deliver glorified victory for the Baylanders. What Korza describes is a real threat, and the weight of the kingdom is on him to succeed.

"You must take the majority of our forces across Jara's Faucet and engage the Valendi from the southwest near Philippia. Push them away from our coordinated retreat, and from our city of Jara, where most of our refugees will be kept safe. Push them, instead, north, and pin them along the river against our city of Wint. With your pressure from the south, the city's fortress along the river will be impregnable. Our pinch will crush these pretenders, and we will drive them all the way back to Hylzar's vile palace in Dor-Eletor."

"I will leave at once to rally your armies, my Queen."

"Make haste, General. The people of our great kingdom are counting on you. *I* am counting on you."

9

A Sight Unseen

Today is finally the day Aris gets to ride out beyond the Orus Mountains. He is practically shaking with excitement, as he has admittedly been a little bored while stationed at the Eastfort. A few training-exercises each day haven't exactly been thrilling. However, it can be said he has been accomplishing his goal of meeting new and interesting people. He and Epi drink every night with the rest of their gregarious platoon and always offer space for additional company, which has made them a quite popular group amongst the garrison. Their hospitality even lured in the Northern Falcon himself, Orvden Liber, for a drink last night. The inebriated Captain tried to teach everyone how to use his signature weapon, the sniper rifle, but he had to stop when literally everyone else in the fort was woken up after enough errant practice shots from their platoon.

Captain Sendis addresses the scouting group at the Panorum Gate. He appears as a silhouette, with the late sunrise fighting through high, wispy clouds in the sky at his back.

"Alright, soldiers, don't get too excited, now." He stares right at Epi and Aris when he says this; the Panorum's proximity to these empty plains lowers their own enthusiasm. "It's an extremely simple scouting mission. We ride out across the Eastern Expanse, cross the River Galantia at its turn, and make our final camp halfway to Mount Galantis itself. We will go no farther, no matter the circumstances. We know what happened to the last group that did." He then smiles and looks over to the scouting party that is to accompany his own.

What sounds boring to Captain Sendis cannot quell Aris's eagerness. The opportunity to see a real volcano is worth the trip on its own.

The other party leader, thirty-five-year-old Tesc Dustin, replies to Sendis sarcastically. "Thank for the reassuring support, Captain."

He then turns back to address his squad. "Let's ride."

Sendis looks back to his group as the others begin their journey. "We are to escort this group and wait for their return after they visit the edge of the forest. We were selected as one of the farthest traveling groups for a reason, as Captain Ben respects our capabilities. Us two are the last scouting parties to ride before he launches his main expedition. Let's not let him down."

And with that, Captain Sendis kicks, and his horse begins to ride out from the Panorum Gate and into the unknown. Before the squad is an endless field of barren grass, looking like a light-brown sea under the morning sun's scattered rays.

Its sheer size is enough to make Aris feel an uneasy awe as he ventures forth into it. He is quite far from home now.

He makes sure to look back upon the towering Eastern Eye as they ride away. From the ground, it looks as if a giant being had come and planted it himself into the mountainside. It's the last beacon of the known world.

Atop this very tower stands Sir Gonder and Sir Jet, basking in the heat of its great flame, which overcomes the frigid air. They look out at the party as they ride away.

"This feeling gets stronger by the day. They should not go near that forest," Gonder laments.

His sentiment confounds Jet. "All the parties have returned safely. I fear your thoughts may betray you. Have you perhaps considered the possibility that your research into the Ancients has biased you on this mission?"

"That forest—it fits what my research, my life's work, has been telling me. The Ancients still live in the east. Think of the knowledge. The opportunity!"

"So that's what you think you will find. Not just more ruins, but the Ancients themselves." Jet finally understands why Gonder was so eager to represent the Inpyrium on this mission, while they practically had to drag him over to the fort.

"They are in hiding. For what reason, I am unsure, but it will take all of our knowledge to handle this situation, to get them to accept and teach us."

"I admire your passion, but it borders on insanity. My senses point me toward a more likely scenario. The scouting party got lost in the woods and died from either starvation or sickness. We should not go near that forest, lest we be subject to the same fate. It's an unnatural place. The Captain said it himself."

"The Ancients' story is not finished, and we shall be the ones to bring it to light."

Gonder turns, steps out of the flame's glow, and moves to return to the fort down the backside of the mountain. Jet remains, still looking out, wondering if his trusted mentor really is insane. If not, his life is about to change forever.

Neither scenario sounds appealing to him.

***

After a long and eventless journey through the plains, across the River Galantia, and around the southern edge of Endendir Ridge, Captain Sendis and Leader Dustin arrive at the rendezvous point in the early morning with their squadrons.

The shadow of Mount Galantis is shading the entire company from the sun. The awesome mountain stands alone, cutting from the horizon through what seems to be the edge of the sky. Though it has not had a major eruption in known history, it is believed to be the sole cause of the infertile plains of the Eastern Expanse. Many even theorize its eruption caused the extinction of the Ancients themselves.

Dustin bids farewell to the group and takes his company farther. The boundary of the forest is said to lie beyond the northern ridge of the mountain.

Aris and Epi, along with the rest of their party, begin to set their tents up in the empty plains. It will only take Dustin's group an extra day to complete the trip, and Aris is committed to spending the entire time waiting with his eyes fixated on the mountain so as to ensure he will never forget its grandeur.

His fixation is interrupted when Epi walks over and addresses him. "I hear we are only a few miles north of the Galantum Desert. Think the Captain will mind if we take a day trip?"

"No chance, Epi," Sendis interjects after overhearing them.

Aris smiles and responds to Epi's question. "I think the only place in the world more boring than these plains is that desert. At least we won't die from heatstroke out here."

"That doesn't sound very boring to me," Epi responds with a laugh.

"Ha! Count me out." Aris laughs. He pauses to think, then continues on a more sober note. "I must say, the sheer size of everything around us has made our home feel quite small. I look upon these wonders and think our life is dull in comparison."

"It's a big world out there; bigger than we can comprehend. Where we fit in it is up to us, but we cannot claim all of it. It's almost taunting."

"Indeed..." Aris glances back to the lonely mountain, then eventually back at Epi. "Do you really think it's up to us? Where we fit?"

"Only if you make it so..." Epi gives a half-smile. "Like when you asked that young huntress on a date at the bonfire."

"Ha. One of my finer moments, if you ignore the brevity of our tumultuous relationship. Although, I must say, it would never have happened without liquid encouragement, along with your own. A better example may yet be when we chased down those robbers outside the market. We received many plaudits for that, enough to bolster our case for admission to the Inpyrium—or, I should say, almost enough..."

"That was a wild one. Quite dangerous when you think back on it, actually. We were lucky those two were unarmed. I can't believe you convinced me to chase them, although I shouldn't be surprised. You have always desired to be the hero of our bedtime stories... Who knows? Maybe out here, you'll get your chance to be a hero. They would have to accept you to the Inpyrium then."

Aris looks at the endless plains around them. "Seems unlikely," he says with a laugh.

"You're right. I am the more likely hero," Epi jests. "I have been practicing my swordcraft with the Panorum. I bet I could cut down a gang of Autoch single-handed if they tried me."

"Maybe, but you're still not good enough to beat me fair and square."

"Ha! Where's our training swords when I need them?"

"I guess we will have to wait until we get home to settle this."

"I am looking forward to it," Epi replies with a wry smile.

***

The next day comes and goes without event.

Then the next.

Dustin has not returned, and Sendis's company's worry grows exponentially by the hour. They lost their line of sight to them once Dustin's scouting party had crossed over the ridge, and the party hasn't been seen since.

The sun is setting. The soldiers begin to prepare camp for another night. Sendis, who has not taken his eye off the ridge all day, turns to the group with a stern look on his face. Behind it, a keen eye can make out fear. "Gather your things. We are leaving."

The soldiers look at Sendis quizzically. How could they leave their compatriots behind? He can sense their tepidness.

"I am under strict orders from Captain Ben himself to wait no longer than a day and a half for their return. I have disobeyed those orders long enough. Those soldiers are in good hands with Dustin. He will ensure they return safely."

No soldier is fooled by Sendis's comforting words. He knows it himself. Something has to have happened.

As few Panorum begin to prepare to leave, a different soldier speaks up in disbelief. "We can't leave them to their doom, sir!"

"We are not a rescue team, Sergeant. We do not know what we are up against. The sooner we alert Captain Ben, the greater chance they have. My order is final. Quickly, now!"

The company hurriedly packs up as dusk begins to take hold over the plains. The sun falls behind the Orus range far in the distance. Aris mounts his horse and looks over to Epi for some sort of reassurance. However, he receives none. The concern of the group has rubbed off tenfold on the two novices, and Epi's confidence has waned.

As the company begins to ride out, Aris takes one last look at Mount Galantis, which is shrouded in darkness, discernable due to its outline blacking out the stars behind it. Its silhouette appears ominous, defiant against the heavens themselves. Along the northern ridge, a low fog has developed, giving the mountain even more of a divine presence.

"Come on, Aris!" Sendis shouts in the distance.

He turns away his horse and hastily joins the others.

10

Xastix's Cradle

It is midday, and a heavy sun now presses down upon Baylander plains. Dust permeates the air as the massive Valendi army marches unchecked over farm and field toward Wint. At its head, Prince Xastix Dumelor, despite his adolescent appearance, rides confidently, adorned in magnetite steel armor from neck to toe, with a black cloak draped over him. Even his horse is heavily armored—so much so that one can hardly discern its white hair. Xastix's own curled hair drapes to his broad shoulders and around his tall figure. He rides as the tip of a black spear, cutting through the light reflecting off the golden plains.

Another rider, wearing just the light-black tunic of a messenger, comes to join him. "General Dumelor."

"What news from the south?"

"The Baylanders have thrown their entire army against our southern legions. Our forces are heavily outnumbered, and Sir Ishitar has ordered a controlled retreat to our position."

"Well, that explains why we have not encountered any resistance. How long until they intercept us?"

"They are marching directly north. That puts the intercept point right on the banks of Jara's Faucet, across from Wint. It is my understanding that you will beat them there by about five days, given the pace of the retreat and your current position."

"Good. That is enough time. Send a message back south informing Sir Ishitar to continue on with his retreat and that his army can arrive no earlier than what we just discussed. The timing here is crucial if we are to be prepared for battle."

"Yes, General." And with that, the messenger kicks and rides hastily away.

Xastix calls forth one of his captains, and she rides up next to the Prince in turn. "Ensure the supply line keeps pace with our army. We are about to pick up speed."

***

Down south, General Medinus sits in loose trousers and a cotton long-sleeve shirt in his tent at nightfall. The Baylander army has made camp after another successful day of driving the Valendi back with little actual combat. Surrounding him are a few of his top officers. He is upbeat. "The Valendi bend at the slightest stress."

"They are woefully outnumbered, and they know it. King Hylzar has lost his mind with this war," the forty-five-year-old General Rudy replies.

"Separated, they are weak, but united, they are a formidable force. They must know this," Ryder insists.

"Not when they are pinned against the river with their supply lines cut off."

"This is what worries me. Why are they so willingly falling into our trap? Wint cannot be taken at the necessary speed, and even if it could be, they would have to find a way to cross the river in the first place, and we know they can't cross it on foot."

"There is no method to this madness," a younger Captain Dagorn chimes in. "They are underprepared, and it shows. It is said Dumelor chose his own inexperienced son to lead the attack, and it's not even the older one, whom I assume he kept back in Dor-Eletor in order to keep him alive."

"Dumelor is many things, but I will not take him for a fool. I do not believe his rise to power was an accident, nor that his days in the Inpyrium were spent idly. He is a threat, and he has proven it already. If he is not walking into a trap, then we are," Ryder asserts.

Rudy interjects again. "There are no traps to be sprung. Our scouts scour the valley behind enemy lines and report no signs of reinforcements heading our way, nor any plots to escape our pinch."

"Then he must expect Wint to fall before we arrive. Tomorrow, we double our pace. We know the Valendi want to retreat. Let's force the issue."

"It will be difficult to rally the men; we have already marched halfway across the kingdom. First to the Zyberian Highlands, and now straight through the middle of the plains," Rudy replies.

"If they can't motivate themselves to save their own people, then they can leave my army and this kingdom, never to be seen amongst the great Baylanders again."

***

Xastix and his legions arrive along the river at night, as planned. Not a single torch is lit amongst the Valendi forces. Instead, they rely on the clear, starry night sky to guide them. The eastern shore is by no means a strong strategic position in the shadow of Fort Wint, which rests atop a bluff along the riverbank. However, years of erosion has caused a raised position right at the corner where the river turns from east to south, giving the area some protection from invaders. The Valendi aim to exploit this position.

"Begin construction immediately," Xastix orders as he stares at the shrouded fortress before him. He speaks loud enough only for his captains to hear.

The message is relayed, and passing through the army's columns come ox-drawn wagons carrying reinforced stone. One-by-one, the wagons are parked to form a rectangle on the small hill, and soldiers begin grabbing the stone bricks and placing them in formation.

By morning, the Valendi plan has been executed.

A fifteen-foot wall now surrounds their encampment, with cannons already placed upon the battlements. The Fort Wint garrison wastes no time in attempting to rectify their negligence once the sun comes up and they see what they have missed. They begin raining cannon-fire down upon the makeshift fort, while the Valendi return fire with little effect from below.

Xastix stands confidently amidst the enemy bombardment, even as bullets whizz past his ears and cannonballs crater into the ground around him. The constant barrage is something the Valendi will have to get used to if they plan on holding the position.

Another captain approaches him on foot. "General, the walls are useless against the towering fortress, and our returning of fire has not deterred them," the Captain says in a panic. "What shall we do?" As he finishes, a bullet flies in and careens off of his shoulder plate with a sharp ping. The force of the impact staggers him for a moment, and its sound startles him.

Xastix takes his eyes off of the fort and gives an unconcerned look back to the captain. "Try not to get hit."

11

The Mist

Captain Sendis's scouting party is charging home to the Eastfort. Aris can hardly hold onto his steed, for they have ridden through the night.

Those standing watch on the Eastern Eye spot the party riding in just ahead of a thick morning mist that has engulfed the rest of the Eastern Expanse. They sound the horn to signal the party's return.

"Good. The final party is back and on schedule. The time for our journey has come," Captain Ben says to Sir Gonder, who has accompanied him for breakfast.

Sendis and his party members cross through the Panorum Gate and eventually move through the front gate of the Eastfort. Once inside in the courtyard, Sendis addresses the group sternly. "Get some rest, soldiers. That's an order. I will debrief the Captain immediately. Those who wish to join the final party to search for our lost brethren may do so. I will certainly be riding." He kicks his steed and takes off up to the keep.

Epi turns to Aris with an exhausted disposition. "I cannot ride a mile further. I think I have had enough soldiering for one lifetime, and we haven't even been in a battle. It's time to go home, Aris."

Aris lets out a wry smile. "Ha, that wasn't too bad. Let's let the real soldiers do the scouting from now on, but I am not prepared to abandon the fort until the mission is finished. We knew what we were signing up for. The least we can do is keep up the garrison."

"You are a true man of honor, Aris. They will tell tales of your bravery back home at the inn for years to come. Ariscles 'Eastfort Garrisoner' Shanis; great name," he replies with good-natured sarcasm. "Fine, I'll stick it out with you here for a few more days."

Up top, Sendis dismounts his horse and bursts into the keep. Several foreign dignitaries, including the two Inpyrian Knights, are in the room. Ben already has his gear on, and looks eager to get on with his journey. "Ah, Captain Sendis—a job well done. Here to deliver your report? Also, if you don't mind, I would like Leader Dustin to deliver it in conjunction with you, as I am very interested in what he has to say about the forest."

"I am afraid that is not possible, Captain."

Ben's face turns grim. The room comes to a standstill. "'Not possible?'"

"Leader Dustin's entire party has gone missing. We fear the worst."

Everyone present sends looks of concern across to each other, except Gonder, who looks unsurprised. Ben continues to press Sendis. "Is it possible they were just delayed?"

"No, sir. We gave them a full extra day to return. A deviation of schedule by that magnitude is highly unlikely."

"You must have ridden overnight, then, to make your schedule."

"Aye. Given the situation, I believed time was of essence if they are to be rescued—if they *can* be…"

Ben pauses for a moment. Successive failures here will surely embarrass the entire kingdom and, not to mention, jeopardize his path to becoming a Panorum General. He gathers himself and speaks with vehemence.

"The Panorum people do not accept nor bow to this mystery in the east. I will take the full Panorum army stationed here to the forest. Everyone else is welcomed and encouraged to join… I will discover the truth of all this."

He turns to his top military leaders. "Inform your soldiers. We all ride at midday."

***

The rallying bells begin to toll across the fort, and controlled chaos ensues as the soldiers hastily prepare for their journey. Just before noon, Captain Ben rides through the fort to check on the status of his force. His chainmail dress covers most of his cloth clothing, and is wrapped over by a worn green cloak. He also dons fingerless leather gloves and boots and carries a rifle and shield on his back and a pistol at his left and right hip.

"The Ordish people will fight with you, Captain," Liber says as Ben rides by.

"The Jyn will also ride with you, Captain," Sergeant Eleshar Fejyn states. As the highest-ranking military member of the Jyn delegation, she speaks for the group.

"The Horventi are eager to prove themselves a great ally," Commander Azen says as Ben nears the base of the fort.

Finally, Ben halts his horse at the Aurelican garrison. "And what of your people?" he asks Skyler.

"Our position remains clear, Captain," she answers confidently. "My soldiers are preparing to go home."

"Very well," Ben replies with a disappointed look on his face. He rides on to the front of the gate to meet Sir Gonder and Jet, with the other forces trailing behind him in long, converging lines.

Gonder confronts him upon his arrival. "Captain, I counsel caution. We do not know what power we are up against. Allow Sir Jet and me to ride forward to assess the situation."

"You are right. We do not... However, I now have the blood of two Panorum scouting parties on my hands. I no longer have time for caution. Let us instead make haste and find conclusion to this once and for all."

Just as Ben is about to begin his trot, an Eastern Eye guard comes racing down the fortress steps, weaving in between riders. "Captain!"

"Oh, what is it?" Ben replies, frustrated, as he turns reluctantly back to the source of the call.

"Captain Landis of the Eastern Eye recommends you postpone your departure."

"What? Why?"

"The dense morning fog has not broken; it now rests upon the walls of the Orus mountains. Visibility from the tower is zero, sir. We expect the ground visibility to be no greater than fifty feet."

Ben is extremely annoyed by this proclamation, to say the least. He gallops out of the fortress alone so that he may look left toward the Panorum Gate himself. Alone in the empty valley between the towering slopes framing the pass, he comes to a stop and stares out at his future. A thick mist is clearly pouring through the gap, obscuring all further view. He scowls in frustration and turns back.

"We must delay our departure!" he announces begrudgingly upon his return. "We will get lost if we leave now. Stay ready!" He looks to the Eastern Eye guard. "Tell your Captain to alert us as soon as the fog breaks."

"Yes, sir."

Ben dismounts his horse and enters the battle command tower, a thirty-foot-tall stone building that lies just across the courtyard behind the gate. There, he plans to wait, ready, until the fog dissipates, while the rest of the force redisperses in the fort.

As the afternoon progresses, this mist rolls in and nestles upon the lower fortress like a blanket. It tickles his skin as he stares blankly forward into nothingness. The last hidden light of the sun falls behind the mountains to the west, and the darkest darkness begins to take hold in the shroud.

Eventually, Captain Ben relents and returns to his keep for the night.

***

When he awakens the next day, Ben quickly glances out his chamber window to find that the mist remains upon the lower fortress, though it has dissipated slightly as it has flowed onward along the Orus Pass. He can now just barely discern the outer wall from his vantage.

Nevertheless, he dresses for travel, hoping the fog will clear, and heads for the keep's main hall. Sir Gonder, along with Sir Jet, awaits him there. Ben speaks first with a cautious tone. "This weather is unusual. We have had fog before, but not like this. The timing of all this is extremely frustrating."

Gonder does not hide his concern. "Something's wrong, Captain. This fog tastes of dust, rather than water. I fear unnatural force works against us."

"Unnatural? What are you suggesting, Sir Gonder?"

"We are not dealing with the Autoch here. This is the work, the power, of the Ancients. They sabotage our journey to the forest because they do not want us to visit. Allow Sir Jet and myself…"

"Now hold on just a minute, Inpyrian. Have you lost your mind? These mythological Ancients are extinct." Ben's annoyed anger is now shifted onto Gonder.

"I am not sure how to respond to that, Captain," Gonder replies, his voice calm but defensive.

"Bad cloud cover doesn't prove the existence of a bygone primordial people."

"All of my research has led me to this moment. The survival of the forest at the base of Mount Galantis proves their magic interferes, especially since the ash of the mountain certainly turns the soil to poison. I will ride with Jet and make contact with the Ancients in the forest."

"As Captain of this garrison, I deny your request. You will ride with us tomorrow, whether it is clear or not."

"Mere soldiers cannot defeat this sorcery. The Ancients' power will destroy you like the others."

"Who said anything about fighting? Or sorcery, for that matter?" Ben walks over to his desk and takes a seat. "As I said, we ride together tomorrow, and this decision is final," he says, waving them away.

The pressure is mounting on him. He has soldiers missing, and he is not one step closer to discovering what happened to Leader Tharmir's party. The mandatory garrison time is near its end, and the foreign force is becoming weary. More and more, he feels his career is at its breaking point. If left unsolved, these mishaps will follow his both reputation and his conscience to his grave.

***

Aris and Epi, along with the rest of Sendis's company, don't mind the break in the action, for respite is much-needed after their hasty return. Now, the night after two days of recovery, the group is back to drinking and socializing with the rest of the fortress, even amongst the thick mist around them. With the drinks flowing, the platoon is able to push their harrowing trip east to the back of their minds for a moment and relax. The two Freelanders drink with each other at a table in the center of a bustling makeshift bar by their quarters.

"Our garrison time will be all but finished once the others leave on the Captain's mission. Do you think we will ever see any of our new friends again?" Epi asks Aris.

"I hope so. Maybe they can come by the Westwood Inn."

"Ha, that's a long way away from Panorus."

"You never know. Maybe we can entice them with a discount." Aris then yells out to the whole bar. "What do you all say!? Would you want free drinks at our tavern!?"

The drunken soldiers cheer in approval, and both Aris and Epi laugh. "See?" Aris says. "They'll all come."

"Very funny. Maybe you can actually convince some of the Aurelicans to show up, since they don't live across the continent, and we'll soon be traveling with them home." Epi pauses to take a sip of his beer, then wipes the foam from his mouth before continuing. "Perhaps you can even beguile the Princess herself. Now that would be quite the guest."

Aris gives a sarcastic look of overwhelm back to Epi and takes a sip of his own drink. "I fear I have not the courage to approach such majesty, nevertheless entreat it. I have only caught glimpses, but what I have seen has captured my utmost attention. Like the north star in the sky, she shines brightest amongst her compatriots, so fair, yet also so imposing that none dare—"

Aris stops in mid-sentence, and a hint of worry begins to show on his face as the rest of the bar slowly stops speaking as well.

The joyous air in the room quickly becomes serious, for a faint-yet-powerful sound of marching can be heard in the distance. The beat's ominous cadence at first is hard to discern, but becomes louder with every step.

In moments, the rallying bells begin to toll throughout the fortress. A distant voice screams out. "All soldiers to their stations! Armed and armored!"

All at once, the soldiers get up and head for their quarters to change and get equipped. Sendis, who was drinking with the group, attempts to control the situation as they move out onto the now-chaotic street.

"We must take our stations, and replace Dustin's stations as well," he orders in a commanding voice. "Sergeant Enther, take the west barracks to our cannon station on the inner wall. I will command the rest of our force on the outer wall in Dustin's stead."

"Yes, Captain... All soldiers living in the western barracks, rally to me when ready!" Enther yells.

This splits up Aris and Epi. Epi will be joining Sendis up front, while Aris will be behind. Frantic, Aris runs back to his barracks to gather his Panorum-loaned armament. He hastily puts on his chainmail, takes up his shield, sheaths his one-handed sword, collects his ammo, and holsters his pistol. Just before he exits, he grabs his rifle, which is the seven-round-clip, bolt-action model that seems to be standard-issue across kingdoms these days, for its efficient chambering technology is much preferred to the barrel-loaded rifles of old. The one difference between the Jyn, Ordish, and Panorum rifles and the others is that their barrels are generally longer in order to provide extra long-distance accuracy at the expense of mobility.

Aris slings his rifle onto his back, takes a deep breath, and then rushes back outside to intercept Epi before they each leave for their company. He finds an armored Epi shuffling through scrambling soldiers on their way to the outer wall. He pats his shoulder from the side to get his attention, and Epi turns to face him. "Well, we wanted to be soldiers," Epi says. He tries to play it cool, but his fear is evident.

"I am not so sure right now."

"It's probably nothing to worry about. I will see you soon," Epi replies, staring reassuringly into Aris's eyes. And with that, the two grasp right forearms, then go on their way.

Aris cannot help but notice the marching has become much, much louder now. He follows Enther up onto the inner wall, to a cannon south of the fort's central's steps. When they arrive at their position, they look out and unsurprisingly see nothing but mist outside the fortress. They can hardly even see the outer wall, which has soldiers stationed five rows back across its entirety. This is a stark contrast to the inner wall, which only has soldiers stationed at each of its eight cannon emplacements.

Enther maintains a stern and collected demeanor. "You two will man the aim; you four will load; I will command when to fire."

Aris is still waiting for his orders.

"The rest of you will be on guard duty. Understood?"

"Yes sir!" the squad replies in unison.

Aris hastily takes position to the right of the cannon some thirty feet away. He lays his shield to rest against the parapet and slings his rifle off of his back. He aims down his sights at the mist.

"Easy there, Aris." A young Panorum soldier by the name of Fiana Telurin pushes down his weapon calmly with a reassuring smile. "We are more likely to hit our own side on the wall than any enemy from here. We have an easy task; we will only have work to do if the outer wall falls, which, of course, has never happened. If it is the primitive Autoch, they won't even have guns or cannons. We won't have much to do tonight."

Aris steps back from the battlements and slings his rifle back over his shoulder. He nods, thanking her for the help, and then looks down at his empty hands to see them shaking violently. He rubs them together in an attempt to calm the tremors.

Captain Ben takes his position atop the command tower by the gate, where he is joined by Sir Gonder and Sir Jet. Skyler takes her soldiers, as instructed, to guard behind the gate, while Commander Azen leads his Horventi forces directly above the gateway. To his right are the Ordish soldiers, and to his left are the Panorum soldiers who make up the rest of the wall's defenses. The Jyn and the Freelanders are sprinkled in with each battalion. The top Ordish sharpshooters, including Captain Liber, sit atop the rooftops of taller buildings within the outer fort to provide sniper support over the wall.

"We can't let them move any further. We must open fire if they are foe," Gonder says to Ben.

"We must wait. The front of the force is almost in range of our northern cannons. If they continue on past our defenses without our approval, they are in violation of Amoria Defense Accords, and we are allowed to engage."

"How can they stop for what they cannot see?"

Suddenly, the marching stops. The silence is more deafening than the marching. As its echo against the mountainside peters out, a light wind becomes audible, and the night's cool becomes more discernible. The air prickles Ben's skin to alert.

"Huh. They must have heard you," Jet says jokingly to Ben.

"If they know our laws, they must be from our kingdoms. Valendi, most likely," Ben replies cautiously.

"It's bold of them to expect passage, given the current political situation in the south," Gonder states.

"Agreed, but it's not unprecedented. I will send an emissary."

Aris stares out into what, with the fog, looks like an abyss. The anticipation is nearly overwhelming him. He gazes down at the southern side of the outer wall, where he can barely make out Epi amongst Captain Sendis's squad.

"What is happening?" he asks Fiana.

"It is an act of war if any force crosses this valley without first receiving the approval of the Eastfort. It must be a Valendi force looking to use the pass. Generally, this would be allowed, but this could be a bit of a complex political situation, since southern kingdoms are at war. I would expect we would let them through and let King Thandus handle the diplomacy."

The idea that it is a Valendi army gives Aris some relief. He again nods and looks back beyond the wall to see if he can make anything out.

Just seconds later, white pockets of smoke protrude from the mist, and are followed instantly thereafter by the loudest sounds Aris has ever heard. It's as if hundreds of cannons have been fired at once.

Then he sees the actual cannonballs soaring in. They smash into the outer wall like a flood of shards and shred the masonry. Some sail over and crash into buildings within the outer fort. Bodies and dust go flying into the air.

Aris looks down in horror to see that Epi and Sendis's spot on the wall no longer exists, as if some giant has come down and taken a bite out of it.

Captain Ben looks on the new ruins of his fortress's defenses in shock. The survivors on the wall are shaken. "Return fire!" Ben shouts at the top of his lungs.

The few soldiers and cannons still upright on the outer wall fire blindly out into the mist. The marching can be heard again, only this time, it sounds like charging.

Ben turns to Gonder. "This fortress is old; it is not fortified with cannon-resistant reinforced stone. We must counterattack immediately if we are to survive."

"Captain, did you just see that? There will be no battle. We are woefully outgunned, and likely outnumbered. You must order a retreat at once!" Gonder urges.

"Retreat?" Ben repeats incredulously. "There is nowhere to go, Inpyrian! Come on!"

With that, Ben draws his sword and begins climbing down the stairs of the command tower. Gonder gives a concerned look over to Jet as they both follow. "There must be another way out of the fort, Ben!" Jet insists, though the booming sound of the gunshots outside the tower makes him nearly inaudible.

"There is one path, but I would only take it in dire circumstances. It's an old trail, likely used by the Ancients when the Orus Pass was covered by a glacier. It is very narrow and precarious. The entrance is near the Eastern Eye."

"Captain, these *are* dire circumstances!" Gonder pleads.

Ben bursts out of the command tower into the gate courtyard. "Not yet," he says, mostly to himself.

A second volley of cannonballs flies in. The top of the command tower is completely blown off. More bodies and debris fall from the wall. Rubble flies in all direction. Ben, Gonder, and Jet make their way to the front of the Aurelican forces behind the gate to find Princess Skyler, distinguishable by her white bracers with blue markings.

Skyler takes her helmet off to address Ben with an urgent look. "What is happening out there, Captain?"

"We have to knock out their cannons," he says to her before yelling out. "Open the gate! Prepare to charge!"

Skyler gives back a most-confused facial expression. "Are you out of your mind!?"

The doormen unlock the hatches, and the gate doors begin to swing open. Despite her trepidation, Skyler replaces her helmet, and the Aurelican forces draw their swords.

They don't even get to take a step.

The enemy has already reached the wall. Four Valendi Knights adorned in black magnetite steel armor and hooded cloaks are leading an unending sea of lightly Valendi armored rabid Autoch soldiers on foot.

Many Aurelican soldiers scramble to sheath their swords and aim their rifles, but they only manage to get one volley in before the enemy forces reach them. The Autoch soldiers smash into the Aurelican line of shields like a wave against a cliffside. Gonder and Jct engage one of the Dark Knights, while another Knight sets upon Captain Ben.

Atop the gateway, Ny Azen looks down at the skirmish and then back up at his dwindling forces, who are trying desperately to lay gunfire upon their attackers, despite the enemy barrages. He knows remaining in place will ensure certain death.

"Abandon the wall! Reinforce the gate!" he commands.

The soldiers are beginning to evacuate the wall when another cannon volley comes in and takes out even more of them. Bodies are torn apart or sent wildly crashing down to the fortress floor with screams of terror. The few panicked survivors, eager to be out of the death-trap of a defense, scurry down to provide support.

Out in the valley, another dark Valendi Knight rides on horseback just beyond the gate amongst the Autoch forces. He is clothed like the others, with armor so dark it's as if its permanently cloaked in shadow, the one difference being that he wears a striking helmet. It has a double-striped comb jutting out at the top of its forehead and a visor that looks as if someone took a rectangular plate, bent it, and cut three vertical lines in its bottom; the middle-bottom vertical line leads all the way to a central horizontal line for the eyes then all the way to the top of the visor, splitting it in half so that it may be lifted around the comb.

This Knight turns to his military leaders and, despite no human in the history of Amoria having the knowledge or ability to do so, communes in the Autoch foreign dialect. The language sounds hoarse, with long vowels and sharp consonants, like a song out of tune and without harmony. "The outer wall has fallen. Move the cannons forward and begin to target the inner defenses."

"My Lord, the gate is gridlocked," General Inuktoch replies.

The officers look the same as the rest of the Autoch army—humanlike figures wearing Valendi thigh-guards, chest-, and shoulder-plates, with some lucky enough to wear visorless helmets. Their main distinction from Amorians is their dirty, rotting skin and withered, scattered hair. This sickly appearance is a debilitating curse that they seem to carry from birth to grave, and the places this disability is worst and most consistently represented is upon the skin of the Autoch's cheeks, their backs, and their calves. Most seem to suffer with every step, and their minds wither every day, as if their very thoughts melt away. Those Autoch least afflicted are given roles of leadership, like General Inuktoch, who is one of the few who manages to sport any significant muscular build.

"If my Knights can't break their lines, then blow your way through," the Knight commands.

"Yes, my Lord," Inuktoch responds, then shouts orders ahead. "Move the bombers into position!"

Back at the gate, Gonder and Jet continue to battle a Valendi Knight. His skills are akin to theirs; he can anticipate their moves before they make them, but he is no match for two highly-regarded Inpyrians. Eventually, Gonder parries one of the Knight's sword swings into the ground, and Jet removes his defenseless head.

Another Knight is distracted in combat when Captain Liber fires at her from his tower, and she is unable to parry the bullet before it enters and exits her neck—a perfect shot just above her shoulder-plate.

Meanwhile, Skyler and the Aurelicans are fending off the initial surge of the attack. Despite the disastrous start to the battle, the gate defense is holding.

Ben isn't doing as well, however. His assailing Knight disarms him by landing a blow directly on his right shoulder and knocks him on his back. Lucky for Ben, his chainmail armor holds up against the strike, although his shoulder has gone numb. He grabs for his left pistol, but the Knight stamps his foot down directly on his arm. The Knight pulls his sword back to finish Ben with a stabbing blow, but he is forced to quickly correct his sword's trajectory to parry a sniper shot from Captain Liber. It gives Ben enough time to recover and grab another pistol out of his right holster. He fires seven shots directly into the Knight's chest and the close-quarters fire rips through his armor and cripples him. Still feeling the effects of his wound, Ben grabs his sword and falls back into the Aurelican ranks.

"Bombers!" an Aurelican soldier screams just a few moments later.

Bursting through the enemy lines are Autoch carrying explosives on their backs and torches in their hands. All Ordish covering fire turns upon them, downing bomber by bomber as they almost reach the Aurelican line.

But there are too many. One finally evades enough shots to reach the defenders.

Boom. The blast takes out the defenders' left flank and sends soldiers from both sides flying, but most importantly, it breaks the Aurelican ranks holding the gateway.

Ben stumbles over in the blast, and is caught by Ny Azen. "We need to fall back, now!" Azen yells at him through the confusion.

Boom. Another blast fills the courtyard.

Chaotic screams erupt around them while stunned soldiers attempt to refocus. The Autoch pour into the fortress. Ben's ears are ringing. He nods, then gives the command. "Fall back behind the inner wall! Fall back!"

Skyler's forces surround her to protect her retreat. Gonder and Jet fight off what Autoch they can as they turn to run as well. In an unorganized panic, all the forces scurry up the central steps to the inner fort. Captain Liber turns to his other snipers and yells out to them. "It's time we be going!"

At that very moment, a new cannon volley comes in and smashes two of the buildings with their snipers still in them, sending the Ordish sharpshooters tumbling to their doom in piles of rubble.

The volley also strikes the inner wall, causing some minor damage. But Liber has no time to grieve for the dead. He rapidly descends his structure.

Aris is now glued to the battlements with his rifle once again at the ready. Watching the battle from afar through the obscuring mist is terrifying. It is an annihilation.

"Faster, faster! Lower your aim—aim for the gate! Fire!" Sergeant Enther screams.

The squadron's cannon shot does little to halt the enemy advance.

Another Autoch volley comes in, and this one is much higher. A flying cannonball misses the squad's own cannon by an inch, but smashes into the stack of cannonballs behind it, sending the iron balls flying. The entire crew manning the cannon is caught in this secondary projectile wave, and are all wounded.

Enther remains focused. "I need the rest of you here to man the cannon!"

Aris runs over with Fiana, but Enther stops him. "Aris, you don't know how to operate this weapon. Keep manning the wall."

Aris nods and scrambles back to his position.

The Dark Knight on horseback rides through the fortress gate and approaches the two surviving Knights that he sent forward, one of whom has been wounded by Ben. "My Lord, he is badly injured," the other Knight reports.

The Knight dismounts. "I have no time for weakness," he hisses. He then unsheathes his sword and thrusts it into the wounded Knight's chest. The wounded Knight lets out a sharp grunt before becoming short of breath and then eventually fading.

"You were supposed to lead the forces forward."

"My apologies, my Lord. I will join the forces at the front."

"There is no need now. I am already here. Look after my horse," the commanding Dark Knight says with anger as he turns and begins to climb the fortress steps.

Soldiers are pouring through the inner gate, and Aris can see the Autoch following in the distance. He aims and fires into the mass, but can't tell if he hits anything. That's when he hears another cacophony of cannon-fire. He ducks below the battlements and glances over to the side just in time to see a cannon ball smash directly into his squad's cannon and hit the black-powder supply. It must've sparked the powder, because the entire gun emplacement explodes in response, sending Aris flying diagonally off of the wall and eradicating the rest of his squad before they can even scream in terror. Luckily for him, the wall is fractionally as high facing in as it is facing out. He skids on the cobbled road before rolling to a gentle stop against a stone house.

After fighting to ensure Liber and his squad have made it inside, Gonder and Jet finally reach the inner fortress just seconds before the gates are closed. They quickly head over to Ny Azen and Ben.

"It's time for us to head for the Ancients' trail," Gonder says.

"I agree," Ben replies defeatedly.

"Good. Take Jet and lead the force away. I will defend the rear of the retreat."

"Very well," Ben agrees before yelling out to the survivors. "All units on me! We are leaving!"

The soldiers rush to the keep. Aris is confused and visibly dazed, but finds a way to fall in with the rest of the army. The passage through the keep is relatively narrow, as only about five across can fit at a time, thus slowing their escape. Ben leads the force into the main hall, then left, to underground steps that lead out to the northern side of the mountain and the pathway to the Eastern Eye.

Just about everyone has made it into the keep when the inner wall gate is blown from its hinges and the Autoch forces come pouring into the inner fort.

Using starlight as their guide, Ben and Jet make their way up to the Eastern Eye. Jet goes to alert Captain Landis of the retreat, while Ben positions himself at the entry point to the Ancients' trail, guiding soldiers one by one around the crest of the ridgeline.

"We will rally along the Ancient Road. Do not stop until I deem it safe!" he repeats as soldiers pass him by.

The Dark Knight bursts into the keep to find no one there. "They have trapped themselves at the Eastern Eye. Very well. They have picked their grave," he says loudly to no one in particular before shouting his next command in the Autoch language. "Kill them all!"

It doesn't take long for the Autoch forces to catch up to the rear of the retreaters. The entrance to the trail is a choke point, but the narrowness of the pass to the Eastern Eye itself allows for Gonder to mount a strong defense. His side has the high ground, and superior numbers no longer give the Autoch a significant advantage. Slowly but surely, they beat back the advance of the Autoch while inching their way to the trail.

There are only about fifty more soldiers left that need to escape when the Dark Knight arrives, confused that victory has not yet been achieved. Fearless, Gonder steps forward to face him as his allies continue to retreat behind.

"Who are you?" Gonder asks in a tone of stern command.

"I am Izedar Dumelor, Son of the Valenor, the Shadow Knight, and the rightful heir to the Kingdom of Valendor, the greatest kingdom in the history of our world. Join me, and together we can take back what is rightfully mine or oppose me, and meet your just fate."

This answer is what Gonder prayed not be the case, but ever since it became clear that it was a Valendi-led attack, he knew who must have orchestrated it. "And so Hylzar's madness finally takes me..." he says to himself.

He wastes no time in swinging his sword at the Shadow Knight, only to be parried as he draws his own blade.

"That was a mistake," Izedar sneers.

The Autoch forces pass by the two of them; continuing to push up against the remaining retreating soldiers. Jet and Ben look on in fear as Gonder duels the Knight.

"We have to help him," Jet implores.

"It's too late," Ben answers as he holds Jet back. Gonder is completely surrounded by the Autoch now. "We need to go."

Gonder and Izedar trade blows back and forth, but neither can best the other. Gonder handles his blade with masterful grace and precision, but his age weakens his pace and force. In contrast, Izedar fights with immense strength and speed, making his defense nigh-impenetrable and his attacks debilitating.

Finally, an opportunity arises to break the impasse. Izedar slips, and Gonder sees his chance to deal a huge blow to the Valendi; a chance to strike down a catalyst of this emerging and evolving conflict. He thrusts his sword forward, only to have the Shadow Knight miraculously recover and evade his blade.

He has baited him.

With Gonder overextended, the Shadow Knight brings his blade up from below and impales Gonder through the chest.

Jet turns away in sadness, while Ben continues to help the last soldiers get through. Other soldiers higher up the trail provide heavy cover-fire for the last few to make it, including Aris, who looks back to see Sir Gonder slumped on his knees. The Shadow Knight raises his blade above his head and thrusts it down into Gonder's neck. Aris quickly looks away in horror and keeps moving. Ben follows the rest of his force up.

The Autoch trying to follow on the narrowing trail are getting slaughtered. The Shadow Knight calls out in Amorian dialect loud enough for the last retreating Eastfort soldiers to hear. "That is enough! Do not follow them to your deaths. We march to Starlinden."

12

MOVING PIECES

A reddened morning sun shines down past the Aldines into Inpyria Valley. Persius Valius, one of the Lords of the Inpyrium, climbs the long, cliffside-chiseled steps behind the Inpyrian Palace in order to ascend to the top of one of the many thousand-plus-foot cliffs that enclose the valley. He wears a formal skinny white toga that stretches down just above his knees with gold embroidered lettering matching that of the Ancients and a gold cloth short-sleeve shirt underneath. For his hike today, he has traded in casual Inpyrian leather sandals that wrap up his shin for their low-ankle leather combat boots. Persius, like all twelve Inpyrian Lords, is quite old, but his health remains strong. He ascends, unencumbered, at a steady pace.

Once reaching the top, Lord Persius never forgets to look upon the beauty that is the Inpyrium. Indeed, it is recognized by many of the kingdoms as the most beautiful place in all of Amoria. Nestled in a valley carved by glaciers long ago, the Inpyrium acts as a home and an academy to those who wish to study not only Amorian subjects, but the lost power of the Ancients as well, for it is one of the few places that remains largely intact from the Ancients' history. The beautiful gold-domed and -roofed gray-marble buildings in the valley serve as a reminder of the great civilization that once was, but was never seen.

Atop the cliff is the crest of Inpyria Falls, a waterfall over a thousand feet high that falls directly into the palace, and next to this crest is why Lord Persius came all this way. There sits a small wooden home, a garden, and a marble gazebo just off the riverbank. Built by the Ancients, this circular structure consists of pillars supporting a gold dome roof and a marble floor with a bowl cut into it. Completely surrounding the edges of the floor are two rows of raised gray-marble benches.

A slender woman wearing a toga similar to Persius's, save for its light blue with white embroidery color scheme, exits the home.

She greets him charmingly. "To what do I owe the pleasure, Lord Persius?" Her hair, all the way down to her hips, dances in the morning's light wind.

"Unfortunately, as you likely suspect from my unsolicited visit, I'm here on business, Lady Quin. The air smells of ash, and the sun loses its white light. I have been tasked by the other Lords to take a look."

"Of course. One moment, please."

Lady Quin goes back inside her home and retrieves a crystal glowing light blue. Referred to by Inpyrians as the Glass, the crystal has a deep connection with all who have touched it. Though its vision can be blocked, it's used to keep watch over all of the Inpyrians spread out across Amoria. If Lady Quin generally knows where a Knight currently is, she can use the crystal to gain their vision.

"Let's have a look, shall we?" Lady Quin leads Persius over to the gazebo, sets the crystal in a small hole in the middle of the floor, and then lifts a lever, thus allowing a small stream of water to flow from the river to create a pool in the floor.

"What have you seen, Quin?"

"Turmoil," she responds sternly. "Amoria is engulfed in war, and our own Knights trade blows against each other in the south. The battle at Wint has become a standstill. The Baylanders cannot break the Valendi's lines, and are now relying on a siege to achieve victory. Queen Korza has set out from Ezebandia, accompanied by her royal guard, though for what reason, I am unsure. We have Knights with her and with General Medinus, who presses his attack from the south. Meanwhile, the Ithorans have made it all the way to the ocean shore, leaving a trail of death and destruction in their path. All of our Ithoran council members ride with the new king, Niike Chutuluru, while our Zyberian council delegation travels with Queen Zila, who has taken the main Zyberian force to intercept her enemy at Telectep."

Persius is disheartened. The peace that has lasted for the prior hundred years is over. "It is disappointing hear that the situation in the south worsens. However, I believe something else is evading us. Have you looked today? Wars have not unsettled nature like this before."

"I check every morning, as that is my duty, Lord Persius. Have a look for yourself."

Keeping her warm charm, Quin steps to the side and raises her arm to welcome Persius forward. He looks into the pool, concentrating hard on the Knights he knows are out in the field. Their sights appear as a faint reflection in the pool, as if he could look up and see what they see above him, rather than the gold dome. One by one, the Glass confirms what Quin told him as it cycles with his focus.

"Hmm, I guess the war is really taking its toll on the world. I will report to the conclave... Wait. There is one other thing. I can't find my friend Sir Gonder."

"Strange, but not unusual. He is at the Eastfort, is he not? The crystal has its limitations. It is hard to see over the mountains. Did any travel with him?"

"Sir Jet, I believe."

"Let's focus our concentration. We will find him instead."

Moments of nothingness pass in the water, and then suddenly, Jet's faintest vision appears. He is not at the Eastfort. Instead, he seems to walk a narrow path high amongst the mountains.

"Where is he? I don't recognize it," Lord Persius says concernedly.

"It must be near the Eastfort. Otherwise, we wouldn't have found him. Wait, we're losing him..."

Jet's view dissipates, and the pool turns back to clear river water.

"What in the blaze is he doing over there? Try to get him back. Pinpoint his location, and inform me immediately as soon as you find him. In the meantime, I must report to the other Lords of the situations in the south. I fear the wars threaten to divide even the Inpyrian Lords themselves. We move toward darker times, Lady Quin."

Persius turns to head back down to the valley.

13

ZILA'S GAMBIT

The war against the Ithorans has been a disaster for the Zyberians. Without the promised aid of the Baylanders, the northern Zyberian forces have been easily beaten back to the ocean shore. The coastal city of Telectep is the last line of defense for the Zyberians before they are completely cut off from the world. Queen Zila Sumptet has ridden out with the rest of her army from Suportep in a last-ditch attempt to save the city. They have made camp upon a ridge just south of it.

Now, Zila stands at the edge of her encampment, staring out over Telectep, adorned in her royal armor. Her armor matches the white iron garb of the rest of her soldiers, save for her gold-painted shoulder-plates, bracers, shin-guards, and helmet wings. She carries her helmet in her left-hand. Its wings signify her rank as an officer; however, the detail of hers in particular—artfully crafted metal bird-wing replicas streaking backwards, rather than just metal plates—identifies her clearly as the Queen. A golden-orange sun sets to her left, giving the petite and short-haired twenty-two-year-old Queen's left side a burning light, while her right is shadowed.

Two camel riders return and deliver their information to General Niles. When finished, the armored general approaches Zila. "What do the scouts report, General?"

"Grave news, my Queen. We are too late. The city has already fallen," Niles says with reserved remorse.

Zila acts unshaken. "And what of the people?"

"It is unclear. The city appears to be empty."

Zila keeps her stare fixed north on Telectep. "General, if the city has fallen, then why do I still hear fighting?"

"What is left of the rest of our army has been pushed back to Telec Point. They have made a makeshift palisade upon an embankment there, and are desperately defending it."

"Did the scouts see how many there are left?"

"Well, it's a bit of an estimate, but they would guess roughly half of our original force."

"That's not enough."

"My Queen?"

Zila turns to the General and responds with conviction. "It's not enough. We are outnumbered, and they control our city's defenses. We cannot defeat this Ithoran force on the offensive."

"But what of your people, Zila? They are surely low on food and ammunition. Are we to abandon them?"

"The army cannot reach them, but maybe the fleet can. Send word to Admiral Fila that she is to begin an evacuation procedure immediately. We will shuttle the soldiers off Telec Point to our position."

"Yes, Queen Zila, but they will have to wait till tomorrow. The shallow's rocks are too difficult to navigate in the dark."

"Very well... And get me on one of the ships. I will be aiding in the rescue."

"My Queen, the rescue will be a very dangerous undertaking. I advise you stay with us."

"This Queen will lead at the front of our lines, not the back... as my father would."

***

The sounds of battle from the city below continue throughout the night. Zila, unable to sleep, stands watching as fires burn below and explosions rattle her people's last defenses. General Niles approaches again.

"Your skiff is ready, Queen Zila."

She dons more nimble armor, her white-leather naval armor instead of metal, and heads for the beach.

Down in the city, Niike grows anxious. He stands atop the burnt-out Telectep town hall with one eye on the battle for Telec Point and the other on the southern Zyberian encampment. He turns to Sir Numenkor. "How are their defenses still holding? It won't be long until the main Zyberian force attacks from the ridge."

"I have moved a significant portion of our forces to the southern wall to brace for an attack. We need only engage the survivors at Telec Point for a few more days before they run out of supplies. Then, they will surrender or die."

"The Zyberians must know this. Why have they not attacked yet if the situation is so dire?"

"I am not sure. Perhaps they just know the truth—that any invasion would be futile."

"The war hangs in the balance. With the complete eradication of their northern armies, the Zyberians are doomed. They have to take action."

Numenkor nods and looks out at the ocean, searching his mind for something he is not accounting for. Then, he actually spots it instead.

"Of course! My King, look over there. A light from a Zyberian skiff just off the coast. Their fleet must be nearby. I'd wager they must be planning an evacuation."

"That is something I will not allow. Have your soldiers divert the cannons bombarding Telec Point to the beach, and cover them with cloth. They won't be able to sail in until morning. Then, when they do, they will be fodder."

***

A humid, gray, windy morning comes, and Queen Zila's resolve has not been shaken. She turns to the Grand Admiral of the Zyberians on the main deck of her ship. "Fila, begin when ready."

Admiral Fila nods and gives orders to launch the operation.

The Zyberian navy is relatively small compared to the larger coastal kingdoms of the New Baylands and Aurelica. The ships are generally two-masted, with twelve light cannons on the starboard and port sides, and two cannons at the bow and stern below deck. Each ship has one skiff on each side. It will take several skiff trips to successfully rescue everyone off of Telec Point.

The fleet emerges all at once around the southern coast, sailing swiftly, unencumbered by any enemy fire.

"We have caught them off-guard. We must make haste before they can rectify their mistake," Zila says to the Admiral.

The ships bob up and down as they shake in the waves of the ocean. The wind moves in their favor; the Zyberians arrive at their destination quicker than expected, and lay anchor just a few hundred feet off Telec Point. "Launch all skiffs! Load as many soldiers as you can!" the Admiral orders.

Zila takes command of one of the skiffs herself, for she plans on seeing this operation through personally. The skiffs are lowered into the ocean, and then begin to row for the shore.

It is only a short row before each skiff arrives on the beachhead. Long-range gunfire persists at the western palisade, and some bullets splash into the ocean near the skiffs themselves. Nevertheless, the trapped soldiers gain optimism, not only from the impending rescue, but from the Queen's presence herself. Their dire circumstances are beginning to look up.

Sir Numenkor and Niike look on patiently from a small sandstone building just off the shore. "All of the skiffs are isolated. Move into position and open fire!" Numenkor commands loudly.

Suddenly, hundreds of Ithorans spring from their city hiding places and onto the beach. They form into groups, each removing the cloth covering the cannons and then manning them.

A wall of cannonballs flies out to sea with thunderous announcement, completely catching the Zyberian fleet off guard. The closest ship to the beach loses both masts and begins to sink immediately. The next two ships catch fire.

"It's a trap!" Admiral Fila screams. She attempts to maintain composure, despite their daunting predicament. "Circle the ships around and get the skiffs back on board! As soon as the skiffs return, we are leaving!"

Zila turns to look back at her fleet in horror. It is way too exposed for that firepower. She looks just in time to see the third-closest ship to the Telectep coast explode. The fire must have caught the black-powder stores. There is widespread panic.

The second volley of cannon-fire incapacitates half of the fleet. The ships are shredded and dead in the water. The soldiers on Telec Point see the crisis in front of their eyes and grow unnerved. Their orderly evacuation erodes, and they all make a dash for the boats.

Zila helps push her now-full skiff off Telec Point as soldiers grab for the edge to hang on. Other skiffs are capsized. It has become a free-for-all. Zila's ship is tipping to the left as soldiers cling to its edge. With no other option, she draws her pistol and fires at them to get them off. "Row us back to the command ship at once!" she manically orders her mariners.

Back upon the ridge, General Niles sees the catastrophe unravelling. "The fleet is completely exposed! Rally the cavalry. We need to take out those cannons!"

He's had the army ready just in case they needed to be called into action, so it only takes minutes for the Zyberian camel cavalry to muster at the edge of the ridge.

General Niles moves to the front of the lines upon his own camel. "Hug the ocean! Stay away from the buildings! We are taking out the cannons on the beach and then retreating! You have your orders! Ride now, and save your people!!"

And with that, he takes off down the ridge toward Telectep, the riders following in silence. Their nerves around their hastily formed mission weigh on their mind.

Zila's skiff is halfway back to Admiral Fila's ship when she sees the camel assault. "No!" she says, exasperated. Her defeat here is looking more and more like it's going to sink more than just her ships.

Moments later, a cannon-shot whizzes in and wipes out one of the soldiers in her boat. All aboard turn in horror as the legs of the body fall to the floor without their torso. "Keep rowing!" Zila screams, her worry fully evident.

Another cannonball whizzes in and does not miss its mark. It hits the skiff directly, wiping out the bow and sending wood shrapnel and bodies flying. Zila tumbles wildly into the ocean as the rest of the skiff tips vertically.

General Niles's riders are within 200 feet of the city when the Ithorans reveal themselves. The majority of the Ithoran army is in position to fire on his force. "Shields up!" he screams.

The Ithoran volley is overwhelming. Thousands of bullets riddle the cavalry charge. While their shields are long enough to protect both camel and rider from the front, they cannot defend from the side as well. It is as if a strong gust of wind has knocked the entire east flank of the charging force over, only they will not get back up.

Niles realizes his mistake, but knows it is too late. "Take the beach! Full charge ahead!" Another volley strikes his force, and many more fall. However, it looks as if some are going to make it.

The Ithorans cannot allow this. At the last second, Niike reveals the final trick up his sleeve. A small strike force of Ithorans, riding on the backs of ferocious jaguars, rush out from the city and onto to the beach, taking the surviving camel riders head-on. The leader of the force is Exzar Osundu, an Ithoran Inpyrian Knight on King Niike's royal council. It was through his Inpyrian training that Ithorans were able to domesticate such savage beasts of their jungle.

Sir Exzar himself identifies General Niles and rides straight to him. His jaguar leaps and poaches the general straight from his mount. Niles only has seconds to feel terror before he is killed as the jaguar devours his noble prey.

The fighting on the beach is fierce and chaotic, but only for a few minutes. The overmatched camel riders manage to take out a single cannon before the rest of the Ithoran army moves in from the city to surround and slaughter the last survivors.

In this time, Queen Zila has swum the rest of the way to Admiral Fila's ship. Fila spots her in the water as they work to rescue what survivors they can from the sea. "Get the Queen on deck, then set sail south!" The crew throws a rope down to her, and she hangs on for dear life as they pull her up. By the time they get her aboard, there are only three operable ships left.

"Go! Go! Go!" the Admiral commands.

The winds have once again shifted in the Zyberians' favor, and now aid their retreat. Fila's ship picks up speed quickly.

"My Queen, are you alright?" she asks while walking over to her.

Zila doesn't have time to answer. The three retreating ships are the only remaining targets for the Ithoran cannons, and with all of the attention on them, they are bound to be hit. A cannonball strikes the command ship dead-on, and Zila is knocked off of her feet.

Fila reaches out her hand and is beginning to pick the Queen up when what seems like fifty cannonballs strike the ship. A piece of wood splinters from the mast and impales the Admiral straight through the heart. She falls directly onto the Queen, inadvertently protecting her from the debris.

Zila is overwhelmed with fear and horror, soaking wet from the sea, and covered in Fila's blood. The ship splits in two with a vicious cracking sound, and she slides back into the ocean just as another one of the surviving ships explodes in a fiery cloud of smoke to her left. Luckily for her, some of the debris falls next to her, and she is able to grab onto a loose board to float.

Queen Zila looks back at the beach, the scattered remains of her fleet, her drowning soldiers, and her abandoned force on Telec Point. A great despair takes her, only dissuaded by her will to survive.

***

It is not until the darkening evening that a small rescue skiff comes upon Zila. Freezing-cold and exhausted, she can't even speak to alert the soldiers that they have found their Queen. Eventually, when the boat is filled with the few survivors that can be found, it returns to the Zyberian camp.

***

Later that night, Zila sits with a blank stare in her tent. Captain Alet Nesten, head of the royal guard and, after today's defeat, acting commander of the Zyberian army, enters Zila's quarters. His presence has often given Zila comfort, as he has been forced to fill the void of the absence of her parents and act as a mentor to the Queen.

But little can comfort her today.

"Queen Zila, I'm sorry to disturb you. As you are well aware, the naval rescue has failed. In order to save our trapped army, we are going to have to take back the city by land. Given the precarious situation on Telec Point, I advise that we mobilize an assault tomorrow morning."

Zila maintains her thousand-yard stare when answering. "There will be no assault, Alet. Have the soldiers break camp tomorrow morning. We make for the capital."

"But, my Queen..."

"The city is lost, Captain. Let's not lose the war here as well, although I am afraid that we may already have. We have no choice but to meet them on the defensive."

"If we fall all the way back to Suportep, we forsake our other cities, and will have nowhere left to run."

Zila breaks her stare to lock eyes with Alet. "I am well aware of the gravity of my decision. There is no other choice."

14

FOE AND FRIEND

A weary-yet-steadfast Xastix walks hastily through mud in the Valendi encampment under heavy rain. Morale is low, but they have held onto their position long enough for the rest of the Valendi army to arrive. With their reinforcements, however, have come the Baylander army as well.

The Valendi's makeshift fort is enough to deter General Medinus from attempting to take their position. Instead, wishing to win without bloodshed, Medinus has ordered the fort to be shelled with mortar-fire. Every ten feet, Xastix has to step around a crater created by the constant bombardment or step over debris and even bodies.

As he arrives at his tent, a shell comes down and smashes into the one next to it, destroying it and starting small fire. A wounded soldier crawls out screaming and engulfed in flames. Xastix quickly unholsters his pistol and fires, ending the screaming for good. He holsters his pistol and continues into his tent.

"I came as soon as I heard you had arrived. How could you have possibly eluded the Baylander siege?"

A hooded figure sitting in the shadow rises to address Xastix. "You don't spend five years at the Inpyrian Academy and not learn how to evade a few patrols." Indeed, it is his father, King Hylzar Dumelor, who stands before him. "You have done well, my son. It is time to put the next phase of our plans in motion. I have personally requested Queen Korza's presence to negotiate peace terms. She will arrive at nightfall, and tomorrow, you and I will meet her in the fort. Are you ready for your new role?"

"Yes, father," he answers with conviction. "Shame. I feel I could have become a great general for you."

"Perhaps, but I am sure you'll find this role more suitable to your comfort. I am placing Sir Ishitar in command of our forces in your stead."

"I promise I will not let you down."

***

The shelling of the Valendi fort abruptly ceases during the night.

The next day, King Hylzar and Xastix walk down to the riverbank to find a rowboat filled with Baylander royal guards waiting for them, along with Sir Baron Stone, one of the members of the Queen's royal council. The guards are adorned head-to-toe in metal armor, just as the regular soldiers are. What distinguishes them is their helmets, which are painted with red stripes, their shoulder plates, bracers, and shin guards, which are all painted red as well, their firearms, which are long rifles with detachable scopes and bayonets, and their body-sized shields, which are black, with one red horizontal and vertical stripe intersecting at the center, and which they wear on their backs. The Inpyrian Knight is armored in dark-brown leather, and has a white long-coat with red embroidery draped over him.

As the two Valendi step onto the boat, Baron grasps for his sword, only to stop himself and relax a moment later. Something about the King emanates power, more so than the average conduit of an Inpyrian, but Baron cannot quite make out what he is sensing.

King Hylzar, dressed in his traditional silk royal garb, nods and smiles at the Knight. "Sir Baron—what a pleasant surprise. I had not realized you had made it all the way up to the Baylander royal court. We crossed paths quite a few times back in the day at the Inpyrium."

Baron is a bit younger than Hylzar, but their times at the Inpyrium did overlap. Dumelor remembers him clearly from a specific time they worked together on a diving expedition in Olovor Bay. They were trying to discover artifacts from the wreckage of the first boats to come to Amoria. Hylzar had his eye on Valendi items, while Baron was focused on Baylander antiques.

The boat begins to row across the river as Baron speaks. "My rise to influence is easily eclipsed by your own, King Hylzar. Sometimes, I wish we could go back to our more trivial research projects."

"Oh, I am not so sure. The world feels simpler to me now than before. Now, if only that meant the world was simple."

The boat reaches the opposite shore, where the retrieval team is greeted by General Medinus, who stands fully armored with distinguishing three-red-striped shoulder plates. "King Hylzar, Prince Xastix—as you are aware, the Queen has agreed to a ceasefire and to meet with you. Please follow me."

General Medinus leads the group, now accompanied by fifty soldiers, into the city. The populace rushes to the main road to get a glimpse of their enemy.

"Don't worry; our people won't dare try anything. We will safely escort you through the city," Ryder reassures them.

The Baylanders keep quiet, but their glares tell another story. There is no love for the Valendi here. The caravan passes many parks now turned into Bandine refugee encampments that sprawl up against brick houses, some of which are damaged from errant Valendi cannon bombardments. Xastix feels uneasy, but Hylzar remains unbothered.

Finally, they reach the fort and head to the main hall, where Queen Korza awaits them. The hall is a medium-sized pentagonal room that sits it the middle of the pentagonal fortress itself. The Queen's royal guards line the walls. While the majority of the room is roofed, there is a pentagonal skylight with stone columns supporting each point. It is under this skylight that the Queen now stands with one of her other Inpyrian advisors, Lady Casey Teth, along with Captain Dunharrow, as the noon sun shines down upon them.

Korza, dressed in her traditional robes and crown, turns to address her visitors. "King Hylzar, you have a lot of explaining to do," she says with vitriol while staring not at Hylzar, but Xastix instead. "I should have you executed where you stand for the plague you have brought down upon our lands."

Dumelor takes a remorseful disposition. "Queen Korza, you must forgive me. This has all been a terrible mistake. An avalanche of misinformation has driven this world into madness. We must—"

"Misinformation?" Korza interrupts angrily, slamming her scepter into the floor. "Was your army misinformed about where your borders lie? I demand you take responsibility for this futile attempt to take power. The Ithorans may have been easy to delude, but to think you could just walk into the New Baylands and claim it as your own because you have an army is not only foolish, but irresponsible. How many lie dead because of your actions? And for what? You couldn't even make it halfway to Ezebandia."

"Queen Korza, your anger and zealousness are understandable. I wish our meeting today could be like old times, when we were both young, and neither of us had to shoulder the responsibility of rule. Tell me, Korza, do you remember when we first met on the archaeology expedition to the Mines of Zerrestra? That man you knew then is the same you know now."

"Those days are long behind us, Hylzar, and I am certainly not the same woman now. I am much wiser, and will not be deceived. All that accentuates your clear betrayal."

"I have not betrayed you or the New Baylands. I only did what I thought was right for my people and my allies. When I received word from the Ithorans that you had attacked them, I panicked. I finally had an ally I could count on. I felt I had secured peace and stability for my people at a time when we were fading. Your invasion struck me as a preemptive move to wipe away our power. First the Ithorans would fall, then us next... I know you, Korza. You have had great ambition ever since we met. I thought, with your legacy at stake, you would secure southern Amoria and wipe out the Valendi once and for all.

"I was wrong. The Ithorans had betrayed my trust; they did not divulge the true detail that they themselves had invaded Zyber, thus prompting your action against them. By the time word had reached my palace in Dor-Eletor from the front lines, your cities had already fallen, and my Commanding General, Prince Xastix here, was surrounded by your army. I had no way to get a message to him. That is why I contacted you, Korza—because you were the only one who could induce the ceasefire. I knew I could trust you."

"So, you are saying that you're not here because of your impending complete defeat, but instead because the cunning King Hylzar has made a catastrophic, rash, and ill-conceived decision to declare an all-out war against the most powerful kingdom in Amoria?"

Hylzar changes from a sorrowful to a defensive tone. "Well, Korza, I don't see it exactly that way, especially your opinion about our impending defeat, but I will concede if that's the first step it takes to move toward de-escalation."

"The first step of de-escalation is your unconditional surrender, Hylzar."

Now Dumelor changes back from defensive to his typical affable demeanor. "I figured you would say as much. If you wish and can afford to have a long, drawn-out war, both here at Wint and in my jagged, tropical mountain home of Valendor, then so be it. However, I think I have a better idea. We sign a peace treaty in which Valendor will admit our fault in the initiation of the war and will provide aid to help rebuild what has been destroyed in your lands. Our entire army will vacate the New Baylands and march back to our mountain kingdom. As a token of good faith, I will leave my own son and Commanding General, Xastix Dumelor, in your custody until our promises have been honored. And, last, but certainly not least, I have a gift for the New Baylands—an heirloom long thought to be lost."

Hylzar reaches under his robes and into a small leather bag on his belt. Both Sir Baron and Lady Casey reach for their pistols, sensing something wrong. Their fear shifts into shock when he pulls out not a gun, but a five-sided crystal glowing dark red.

The whole room is frozen for a few moments.

"It cannot be... the Amorian Star!" Korza says, stunned, ignoring the rest of what Hylzar has proposed. "Long did the New Baylands kingdom prosper as their leaders wore this crystal upon their heads. Long has the royal family suffered without it... How? How have you found it?"

"Well, I am afraid it has been in my possession for quite some time, although it wasn't until just recently that I discovered its true importance. Back when I was still conducting archaeological research on behalf of the Inpyrium, I traveled out to the site of the Battle of Galantum, where the southern kingdoms permanently pushed back the Autoch invaders once and for all. While the battlefield has been covered with the literal sands of time, my in-depth knowledge of the event allowed me to pinpoint the exact location of the fighting. I uncovered many artifacts that were significant to historians, but all-in-all, it was a pretty unexciting trip—that is, until I found this crystal. Though it was cracked, I still sensed a great power emanating from it, and so I took it for my own to study. Unfortunately, I wasn't able to gather much information at all from it, and I could never harness any power from it. As time passed, it lost my attention, and soon, I was forced to move on to what you could appreciate was more pressing at hand—leading Valendor. It was only by chance that when I was showing it off to a few visitors to my court, one of them suggested it could in fact be the Amorian Star, based on what he had seen in old paintings in Ezebandia. With this new thought in mind, it didn't take much time for me to do more research and connect the dots. I was hoping to give it to you at my palace in Dor-Eletor as part of a grand celebration of a new beginning between the Baylanders and the Valendi, but you rejected my many invitations."

Queen Korza walks out of the skylight and slowly toward Hylzar. The room is tense. When she arrives, she looks him directly in the eyes and then down at the crystal. She stares almost with lust at the object as she slowly reaches her hand out and takes it from him. Dumelor gives an assuring smile back at her.

In a moment that seems to last forever, she continues to gaze at the crystal now in her grasp. Finally, she looks back up at him. "I will consider your proposal and give you an answer first thing tomorrow. In the meantime, Xastix will stay here. If we reject it, he will be returned. However, I will be keeping the crystal no matter what."

"It was a gift, Korza; of course you should keep it. I understand your need to think this over. I look forward to your answer."

"Ryder, escort Hylzar back to his camp. Baron, Casey, take Xastix to an empty room. Jof, I want royal guards watching that room at all times."

The crowd in the room disperses. Hylzar looks over to Xastix and gives him a reassuring nod before the Prince is whisked away by the Baylander Inpyrians.

Korza's gaze shifts back to Xastix and does not break from him until he exits. She clutches the crystal tightly.

***

Later that afternoon, Queen Korza gathers her present royal council. On the council today sit General Ryder Medinus, Captain Dunharrow, Sir Baron, and Lady Casey. Lady Casey isn't over the age of thirty, but the Queen trusts her, both as one of the top Baylander Inpyrians and as the daughter of Aria Teth, the Queen's longtime friend, who passed away from sickness when Casey was only eight years old. Korza treats Casey as much as a step-daughter as an advisor.

Missing from the council are two additional Inpyrian Knights, along with Admiral Kent Walsh, several economic advisers, and Korza's husband, Rodrick Amoria, a retired businessman and a member of the prestigious Keller family, whose wealth can be traced back generations, even to the old world, due to their prosperous shipping company. All those absent have been left in Ezebandia.

The present council members sit at a table set up in the main hall of Fort Wint, where the meeting had taken place earlier. "Queen Korza, if I may?"

"Go ahead, General Medinus."

"We have the Valendi army right where we want them. To allow them to retreat unimpeded would be a mistake. King Hylzar is right when he says that his army is not near defeat. Their position is strongly fortified, and they have suffered limited casualties. However, with time, morale will begin to fail as their losses pile up with no victory in sight. No one can predict how many will die before the will of the army breaks, but I can assure you, with our current siege, their losses will begin to grow exponentially. Don't be fooled—once the Valendi army falls, there will be no struggle to march into the southern Orus mountains and take Dor-Eletor. Valendor simply does not have the populace to resist our might. Dumelor knows this. Today was his last effort to save his rule."

"While I agree with your assessment of the war, General, I am not sure I agree with your course of action. To be caught in a prolonged war here means we are vulnerable everywhere else. The Ithorans will destroy our ally to the south. Our economy will be crushed, and our citizens will starve, as half of our fields will not be worked. Our cities will continue to flood with refugees. Not to mention, our northern border will be completely unprotected from an Aurelican invasion."

"They wouldn't dare, my Queen," Captain Dunharrow interjects.

"Are you so sure? An Aurelican fleet has been spotted by our spies sailing down the coast of the Freelands as we speak."

"Merely an empty show of force," Jof dismisses quickly.

"Maybe so, but I will not give one window for our enemies to strike."

"Then it seems you have already made your decision, my Queen," Ryder responds.

"Not quite. We need to be certain the Valendi will hold up the end of their bargain, which leads me to my greatest concern. Where is Hylzar's firstborn? Shouldn't he be leading the army?"

Sir Baron now chimes in. "It's unclear what has happened to Izedar. Our spies say he has vanished, although Dumelor has not seemed to acknowledge it. Izedar is widely accepted as the favorite son of King Hylzar, so Xastix's appointment as commanding general over Izedar was certainly unexpected, further advancing the questions around Izedar's whereabouts, or perhaps his health."

General Medinus follows up. "Even so, young Xastix has done a formidable job leading the Valendi forces, though his mission was doomed from the start. Perhaps that is why Izedar was held back and Xastix was left with us. King Hylzar was already resigned to his fate of losing Xastix in this war."

"But he needn't have sent any sons if he knew the probable outcome," Dunharrow counters.

"Unfortunately, Xastix's presence here is more dangerous than you all know. It was no mistake that he was left with us. Hylzar seeks to manipulate my emotions against my better judgement. He has always been good at it..." Korza says the last sentence with a regretful tone. She pauses to think, then changes the subject. "What of the crystal? Do we believe his story that he didn't know what it was when he found it, or even how he found it?"

Sir Baron is the expert on this matter. "It is possible. While there was knowledge as to the fact that the crystal was missing, where or when it was lost is not in our records at the Inpyrium. Finding a crystal there would not necessarily have led anyone to believe that it could in fact be the Amorian Star. Especially since it was found outside of Baylander territory."

"Then I believe him. Only the royal family knew the crystal had been lost when King Lender Amoria was wounded in the Battle of Galantum. We had sent several archeology expeditions in secret to try to recover the crystal, but had been unable to correctly locate the ancient battleground. My family gave up hope of finding it long before I was born." Korza stops for a moment and lets out a sigh. "The Hylzar I know would have never made this clumsy invasion, but he also would never betray me like this, either. We were very close years ago—dare I say, too close. I must do what is best for all Baylanders and return our lands to peace. It is not the time for conquest, for we have too many enemies. Valendor has been taught a lesson for now. Perhaps in the future, as our power grows, we can finally snuff out their hold over us in the east for good."

Korza then stands and exits the room.

***

It is now evening. Korza sits alone in her high chambers in the fort. The last bit of the day's light shines through a small open window. She takes off her crown and stares at the empty space where the crystal once laid.

"I will bring glory back to my family and my people." She speaks softly, but with determination.

She pulls out the Amorian Star. The crack across its center does dim some of the crystal's beauty, but Korza is unconcerned. It is the power within it she chases. She sets the crystal back into her crown and places it upon her head. A strength the likes of which she has never felt before instantly runs through her veins. Out of what feels like instinct, she walks over to her desk and grasps her scepter.

Korza thinks to herself as she stares out the window. *The Amorian Star and Flame united once again. A power that shall reshape the world.*

The strength of the crystals is making her feel a little light-headed, but she refuses to take them off. Eventually, she ends her indulgence in future reveries, and decides it's time to interrogate her new captive Prince.

***

An empty storage room in the basement of the fort has been hastily converted to chambers for Xastix; it just contains a bed for him with no windows. The Queen enters without knocking.

"Queen Korza. To what do I owe the visit?" Xastix asks innocently upon her arrival. He's sitting upon the bed.

"My need for answers, young Xastix."

"I am afraid I don't have many beyond what my father has told you, but I am happy to try to help."

Korza smiles. "Guards, leave this room at once." she orders sternly.

The two guards stationed by the door exit without hesitation. They don't dare defy the Queen, despite the risk of the command. Xastix is surprised by this decision, but knows he will not move against her.

When the door is shut behind them, Korza continues. "I do not come to discuss Valendi politics. I come to discuss you. Why has your father brought you here?"

"Queen Korza, forgive me if I sound discourteous, but isn't it obvious? I am a member of the royal family and the commanding general of the Valendi army. Leaving me with you gives weight to my father's promises."

Korza stares deeply into Xastix's eyes, as if trying to unlock them with her mind. "Where is your older brother?"

Xastix returns a confused stare. "He remains in Valendor. My father is training him to become King, leaving me with the responsibility of commanding the army."

"Hylzar doesn't fear that your popularity in the army may erode Izedar's support and allow you to usurp him?"

Xastix grins. "Queen Korza, such a heinous act may be considered in other families, but not in ours. We are tight-knit; loyal to our kingdom, not our own ambition."

"I can see how you three's relationship would be close, especially with the fact that you have no queen." Korza finally gets to the question she needs answered. "Tell me, Xastix, who is your mother?"

Xastix now appears shaken and irritated. "I do not see how this is relevant."

Korza doesn't respond. The room is silent for a five-second eternity.

Xastix gives in. "The circumstances around me and my brother's birth have always cast a shadow on our reputations, despite that having zero effect on our legitimacy. It is always foreigners who throw the most unfair judgments upon us and our father. The truth is that Hylzar has never told us who our mothers were; only that they were killed in the poisoning attack on the royal family. The memory is very painful for him. We do not press him on it, nor do I wish to carry my thoughts there, for the absence of her in my memories brings me melancholy."

"So, even you do not know... Hylzar's right hand keeps his honor, while his left deceives." These words are aimed more at herself than Xastix. Korza stands and places her right hand on Xastix's shoulder. She keeps her gaze, but now, her face reads of sorrow. "You cannot stay here. You will be given back to your father immediately, never to return to our lands."

Xastix is nervous. Now is his fateful moment. Mustering what menace he can conjure from his spirit, he locks eyes with Korza, stands, and grabs her right shoulder aggressively; mirroring her own action upon him. She is startled by the move.

"I am afraid, for all of us, things are in motion that cannot be undone," Xastix says firmly. "My place is now at your side."

Before Korza can let out a scream for help, she begins to fade. Fear ravages her, but she cannot speak, for she feels petrified by a surge of power flowing through her. It's as if Xastix stares deep into her very mind. The Amorian Star's light glows brightly and reflects off Xastix's pupils.

Slowly but surely, she loses consciousness.

15

RUIN

The sun has fallen behind the western horizon of the Orus Mountains as the survivors of the Eastfort garrison press on. The silhouettes of dense clouds across the sky are backlit brightly, while the clouds themselves are dark. One of these clouds is now directly overhead, and a thick snow gently begins to fall.

The soldiers march single-file, as that is all that fits on the precarious trail. Their faces tell the story of the battle they've just lost, and weariness threatens to overpower their already-fading morale. The front of the column is led by Captain Ben, with Sir Jet Ikonobo slightly offset beside him.

Ben glances up at the sky. "A spring snow... and just when I was starting to believe things couldn't get any worse. If this gets heavy, the Ancient Road will be untraversable."

"The Ancient Road, Captain?" Jet asks.

"Aye. When the Panorum settled these lands, we discovered this trail used by the Ancients while the Orus Pass itself was covered by a massive glacier. It leads all the way to the Shimmering Sea. From there, we surmise they used the Alcyon river to cross Amoria."

"Well, I am very thankful it takes us exactly where we want to go. However, I am not sure we will ever make it at this pace. What's left of the garrison is tired, and I doubt our ability to traverse this primeval trail in the dark."

"I agree, Sir Jet. If my history books were accurate, we should be coming up shortly on an old Panorum outpost by the name of Ilantum. Initially used as a watchtower over the Orus Pass, it was abandoned after the Autoch were pushed out of the Orus range and the Eastfort was constructed. Hopefully, we can make camp there."

Near the very back of the retreating column is Aris. He sports nothing but a bloodshot blank stare on his face as he trudges up the trail. Though he remains with the survivors, he can't help but feel alone. His entire company was massacred in the attack, and his lifelong best-friend had gone up in smoke within seconds of the start of the battle. Their adventurous excursion has turned into a nightmare that he now feels he will never escape.

If only we had just stayed home... he thinks to himself, imagining the peaceful town of Baywood—the small waves crashing on the beach, the lights and laughter emanating from each household. *We gave it all away...*

The front of the line circumnavigates the corner of a ridge, and there they see it. Perched on a wide plateau just about a hundred feet below the mountain's peak sit the ruins of the Ilantum Outpost.

"There it is," Ben says with a hint of relief in his tone. "We make camp here tonight!" he announces to the column.

The stone outpost consists of several one- and two-story stone buildings now crumbling in decay. The buildings sit on a rectangular ridge with the mountain curving around it on all sides except for its north. On the north side is a twenty-foot cliff leading into a sharp snow-covered slope that drops all the way down into a frosted-white valley. To the south of the outpost is the mountain's peak, where one can make out a small stone watchtower flanked by cannons also facing south.

Jet spots the tower. "This outpost is on the wrong side of the ridge. That tower must be the vantage point they used to watch over the road."

"Let's take a look," Ben replies.

The two find some stairs carved into the side of the mountain in the middle of the outpost and make the short climb to the tower. The tower stands just around twenty-feet tall and serves no real purpose except to shelter its inhabitants from the harsh weather. Nevertheless, the two climb the few steps to the top and peer down to the Orus Pass to see if they can spot the Autoch army.

"I don't know what I expected," Jet says disappointedly. The valley is completely eclipsed by mist in both directions.

Ben looks east and can see the Eastern Eye still burning on the horizon. "The flame will die soon without a crew to maintain it. That flame has never gone out since the tower was built hundreds of years ago," he laments.

Jet reassures him. "Have faith, Captain. The light of our people will not be so easily snuffed out."

The two descend back to the outpost, where now, the entire retreating force has arrived. Ben shouts orders to the group. "Make shelter in the ruined buildings and get fires going! It will be a cold night. I want a constant group of guards watching the trail—the enemy could be following us! And I want a meeting with all of the leaders immediately."

"Captain!" a Panorum sergeant interrupts Ben's spree of directives and approaches him. "You should see this."

Ben is led to a large one-story building with a decayed wooden roof. "I don't think we will be starting any fires in this building, Captain," the soldier says as they enter.

Ben walks in to find the entire space filled with black powder and munitions. "They must have decided to leave it behind when they abandoned the place. Tell everyone to restock here. We're going to need to be fully supplied to defend Starlinden."

"Yes, sir."

Ben walks from the building to the ruins of the captain's quarters, where he finds Jet, Princess Skyler, Commander Azen, and Captain Liber. "Where is Sergeant Fejyn?"

"It appears Eleshar was killed in the battle, Captain," Azen replies.

"Understood." Ben pauses and then continues. "I will assume command of the surviving Jyn and Freelanders. In the meantime, how many survivors were there? I count 232 Panorum."

"I have 176 Horventi left, Captain," Azen replies.

"There are seventy-two left of my force," Skyler adds.

"I count 121 Ordish," Liber says. "The Jyn were almost completely wiped out. There are around thirteen survivors."

"And does anyone know of the Freelanders?"

"I only know of one, sir. Apparently, his Panorum battalion was killed," Orvden replies.

Ben sighs. "The Freelanders were completely out of their depth in this battle."

"We all were, Captain," Jet responds.

"I can't deny that. If someone could find him for me after this meeting, that would be greatly appreciated. I will take personal responsibility for him out of respect for his people. In the meantime—the main reason I called you here. I must ask... Panorus is under attack. Our capital stands in the path of our enemy. Will you defend it with me?"

The room is silent. Ben shows desperation. "You must know if Starlinden falls, your cities will be next!"

Azen finally speaks up. "There has already been so much loss, Captain. We all need to return to our homes and regroup. We must unify our forces, our real armies, if we hope to stand a chance to defeat this enemy."

"And in doing so, you likely guarantee my people's demise."

"I cannot tell you what to do, but when we arrive in Starlinden, I suggest you evacuate the city. Either retreat to another one of your strongholds, or seek refuge in our cities. Together, we can save the world from this terror."

"Even if I agree to do such a thing, King Thandus never would. You ask the impossible."

"He must be convinced. Otherwise, everyone in that city will die."

"Think on it, Azen. All of you. I beg you. Do not abandon us," Captain Ben pleads.

The other leaders nod and exit.

***

Some time passes before Aris arrives at the captain's quarters. Night has now completely fallen on the outpost, and the building's main room is now lit by a small fireplace.

"Captain Liber mentioned you wanted to see me, Captain?"

Ben, while still tending to his fire, looks up to greet Aris. "Ariscles Shanis—the last surviving member of the Freelander garrison at Eastfort. I am so sorry."

"I appreciate that, Captain. This ordeal has been tragic for all of us. I...I am not sure any of us will ever be the same. At least, I won't." Aris tries to keep himself together, as this moment of reflection reminds him of the loss of Epi.

"Indeed," Ben responds. "Now, we must move our focus on to ensuring that we get to, in fact, live out the rest of our lives, altered or not. That is why I am naming you my personal bodyguard for the rest of the mission to Starlinden. I am counting on you to protect me from all threats, whether they come from our enemy or within."

Aris is caught off-guard and confused by the offer. "Captain, thank you for this honor. However, I am not sure I am the most qualified for this position."

"Maybe not... but it is your position now, nonetheless. You will make my quarters your home as well tonight, and will stay by my side at all times. Understood?"

"Yes, Captain. You can call me Aris, by the way."

"Good. Now get some rest, Aris. I will wake you before sunrise, in the early hours of the morning, and you will take your post guarding me. If anything feels wrong, alert me immediately."

Aris nods and shuffles off to make a bed for himself. The captain's quarters are small, but have a second room that can be slept in, along with some stairs that lead to an observation deck on the roof.

Captain Ben walks over to an old stone table. On the table sits a map that he has drawn from memory of Starlinden and the surrounding area. His mind races through a thousand scenarios for the impending battle and how the Panorum can defeat their Autoch invaders. For so long, he had dreamed of rank and distinguishment, but now those desires are foreign to his mind. His position, and the weight of it, has become all so real to him, and he agonizes over how he can save his home and his people. At least those he has not already lost.

***

At roughly three in the morning, Ben wakes Aris. "Your turn, Aris. Wake me at sunrise," Ben says as he lays himself to rest.

Aris puts on his chainmail armor, grabs his sword and rifle, and walks up to the observation deck of the captain's quarters. A light snow still persists, but it looks like they have avoided a serious blizzard. Dying fires glimmer throughout the outpost, and the entire camp is quiet, save for a few soldiers assigned to the rear-watch chatting by a fire. The whole group is exhausted and taking advantage of their first real rest since their catastrophic defeat at Eastfort.

Aris goes over and sits on the ruins of a stone bench on the roof. He looks out, but cannot see far. Clouds above obscure most stars.

Quickly, his thoughts betray him. They are filled with fear and anguish. His mind harkens back to when he and Epi were younger, sitting on the beach and letting the tide run up against them. They talked about their dreams, about what they would accomplish in life when they were finally able to escape their town. They ranged everywhere from becoming Inpyrian Knights to becoming simple traders who traveled through and experienced all of Amoria. It had never been a matter of if, but when, and they'd always agreed that they would do it together.

Aris wonders what he will tell Epi's family if he ever gets out of this mess. He had died chasing his dream, but it was not a heroic death, like they had read in their favorite stories, but one of impersonality and insignificance. Indeed, it feels like his life was all for nothing, and that hurts Aris even more. Whatever is to become of his own life, he fears he will always be alone without Epi by his side.

That desolate feeling sends chills down his spine, and he snaps out of his thoughts to escape his pain... or at least, he tries to. The outpost feels even quieter than before, for it is.

He looks over to the rear-watch to see their fire extinguished and the soldiers nowhere in sight. His existential fears turn into something more palpable.

He rushes back down into the captain's quarters and awakens Ben. The drowsy Captain stumbles over to grab a spyglass, then heads up onto the observation deck to take a look.

"I don't see anything at their encampment. Where in all the Orus are they?" He scans to the nearest fire to them.

"Everything looks fine there...wait..." Captain Ben sees a glimpse of something, or someone, he doesn't recognize, and then the fire is snuffed. "Ambush!" he screams at the top of his lungs.

As if he's set off a bomb, loud bangs of gunfire ring out from the eastern camp.

The Autoch have followed them to the outpost.

"Hold position here while I dress! Then we must repel the enemy," Ben says to Aris as he frantically makes his way back downstairs.

Aris looks back over and can't quite make out what is happening in the dark. However, the sounds fill in what his eyes cannot discern—gunshots, the clashing of swords, and screams permeate the air.

Ben returns to the roof moments later. "Let's go, Aris."

The two make their way down and out of the captain's quarters; Ben bursting with energy, while Aris follows more timidly. Their eyes meet a fearful Skyler. "Captain! What is going on?"

"The Autoch are here. We need to hold their attack at the entryway. If they make it far into camp, we will be overwhelmed. Where are the other leaders?" Ben replies with frantic determination.

"They must have already pushed forward."

"Then we must join them!" Ben signals to what soldiers he can see around him to follow, and the group breaks into a jog east. They weave through the ruins and pick up more soldiers as they go, with sounds of battle getting closer and closer.

"Watch out!" a Panorum soldier screams as a wave of Autoch emerge from the dark and smash into the group's right flank. Aris draws his sword at the last moment and wildly slices through a stumbling Autoch soldier who had penetrated the group's lines.

"Protect the Princess!" an Aurelican soldier yells as their forces form a circle arounds Skyler.

Ben draws a pistol and guns down several Autoch before they are upon him. He unsheathes his sword with his left hand to block an Autoch swipe at his side, then bashes its head in with his pistol grip. Many of the group are felled around Ben and Aris before they finally feel some respite from the initial attack.

"We need to push forward!" Ben yells as more friendly forces join them from the western side of the camp.

"Fall back!" a voice screams from just up ahead. In a few moments, Commander Azen emerges with Jet following behind, protecting their retreat. Azen is covered in blood, though it looks as if none of it is his own.

Ben intercepts him. "Commander, we need to push them back!"

"Captain, we are overrun."

"We don't have a choice. Where is Orvden?"

"He had his group take sniper position on top of the ridge," Jet answers over Azen while parrying gunfire.

Ben now addresses the entire group. "All of you, with me. We will cut a hole directly to the eastern entrance and plug the flow of the enemy. Charge!"

They make it all of fifteen steps before they meet the full brunt of the attacking Autoch forces, but Ben is unshaken. He cuts down several Autoch quickly, inspiring the group to keep pushing.

Up on the ridge, Orvden and his best shooters gun down the unsuspecting Autoch from above. With the surprise attack revealed, many Autoch now carry torches into battle, thus making themselves easy targets for the Northern Falcon. However, there are just too many. Orvden can see Autoch already halfway through the outpost. The fighting is spread-out and chaotic. It is hard to discern who is winning.

Back down below, the main group commanded by Captain Ben has made some progress east, but they have also been funneled north toward the cliff's edge from the enemy's pressure. Ben is okay with this. With their left flank protected by the cliff, they are able to mount a better offensive forward. As they push ahead, they pick up more allied soldiers as well.

Peering through his sniper scope atop the watchtower, Orvden clearly sees Captain Ben and his forces. "Ben's group is advancing." He turns to the two other snipers in the tower, Devden Skip and Raya Alsten. "Concentrate all your fire on enabling their progress. We ain't lost yet."

An Ordish voice screams from below on the ridge. "Captain, the stairs!"

Orvden turns to look at the stairs leading to their position. Unlit shadows climb them. He can't quite make out if they are friends or foes. He makes a tough call. "Shoot 'em down!"

It's too late. A few Autoch are downed, but many still pour onto the ridge. Orvden swings his rifle onto his back and draws his pistol and one-handed axe. "Stay focused on Ben's group," he orders Skip and Raya, then makes his way down and out of the watchtower.

While he earned his nickname, the Northern Falcon, due to his ability with his rifle, there are none in all Amoria who match Captain Liber's skill with the pistol-and-axe combo. Famous for putting down town insurrections in Ordenwood, Liber's reputation for being one of the most revered warriors in all of Amoria shows in the battle now. His shots don't miss the Autoch's heads, and he easily out-duels any enemy who reaches him.

Just when Orvden believes he has defeated the attack for good, a new tall, shadowy figure emerges from the mountainside stairs with more Autoch trailing him. The Autoch rush to challenge the other Ordish soldiers, completely disregarding Captain Liber. With a hint of dawn now breaking the darkness on the mountaintop, the figure is revealed—the Shadow Knight. Orvden fires all seven bullets he has loaded at him, but the Knight parries each shot with his sword, with the last flying back at Orvden and clipping his right arm.

Orvden screams in pain and drops his pistol. Now wielding just his axe and adrenaline, he charges the Shadow Knight, swinging his axe in a one-handed overhead attack, which the Knight easily parries away, as Orvden predicted. He then makes his real move—a full 180-degree spin counter-clockwise while drawing a dagger from his belt with his aim aligned for the Shadow Knight's neck. The move happens so fast that most who have faced it in the past have died before even knowing their own cause of death, but the Shadow Knight's reflexes are much more attuned than those of an average soldier. He catches Orvden's left arm before he can land the blow and, with Orvden's axe now on the wrong side of his body, he has no way of preventing the Shadow Knight's downward strike, which removes his arm at the shoulder.

Captain Liber is in too much pain and shock to react in time to the Shadow Knight's following swipe from below, which cleaves him from hip-to-hip. Liber's body, now cut into three pieces, crumbles to the snow-covered ground.

The Shadow Knight steps over his mangled work and makes for the watchtower as the rest of the surviving snipers battle hopelessly against the overwhelming Autoch on the mountain top. Meanwhile, Skip and Raya remain focused on the battle below, as ordered. The Shadow Knight reaches the top of the tower and, before either of them realize what is happening, stabs Raya through her back. She screams in horror at the sight of his blade protruding from her chest.

Skip panics and jumps from the tower before the Shadow Knight reaches him and crashes into the snow. He rolls out of control all the way down into the outpost before coming to a stop. Dazed, he gets up and runs for the one group he knows still has a fighting chance: Ben's.

Skip's run through the dawn-shadowed outpost is harrowing. There are bodies and fighting everywhere. There are no lines in this battle, only chaotic one-on-one combat everywhere he looks. He is jumped by a few Autoch attackers on his way, but he is able to best them with his axe.

By the time he reaches Captain Ben and the others, their group's advance had been halted. He can hear Jet yell out. "Captain, we've lost our momentum, and we are no longer getting sniper support. We need to make for the western pass."

Ben breathes heavily after he shakes off another Autoch attacker. "I believe we cannot outrun them, but I also see there is no other choice... Make for the western exit!" he screams to the survivors.

Still fighting, the group carefully falls about halfway back through the outpost before they encounter resistance from the west as well.

"We're surrounded!" a soldier screams.

"Push through!" Ny Azen urges.

The group's resolve will not be denied, and they begin to make progress, despite the Autoch pressing them from all sides. Just when hope seems no longer out of the question, Ben sees a building on his left, fifty feet from him, engulfed in flames.

That's not possible, he thinks. *All these buildings are stone.* Then he recognizes it: the armory.

"Get away from the munitions!"

Everyone turns and tries to run closer to the cliff's edge, but it's only a few moments later that the whole place erupts. The explosion from the black powder inside finally gives a sun to the dawn sky, its fiery orange light illuminating the entire mountainside. The center of the outpost is completely destroyed. Stone debris flies in every direction, killing both Amorians and Autoch.

Aris is caught in the shockwave and thrown from the ridge. He smashes down below on the snow-covered mountainside and tumbles uncontrollably all the way to its base.

16

THE TURN OF THE TIDE

Queen Korza awakens in her bed to a cloudy morning at Fort Wint, absent any thought or memory of what occurred the night before. She feels not quite herself, but forgets all about it when she sees the Amorian Star resting in her crown.

The legend of the crystal runs deep within her family. It is believed that the crystal-infused crown imbued them with higher intelligence, discernment, and leadership ability. For centuries, it had guided the royal Amoria family through the trials and tribulations of establishing a new home across the ocean. The crystal's loss had coincided with the New Baylands' stagnation, and was eventually followed by their "defeat" against the northern kingdoms, thus costing them what is presently known as the Freelands.

Now, Queen Korza believes that the emergence of the Amorian Star coinciding with their own rise back to power is no coincidence. She hastily gets out of her bed and nestles the crown upon her head before she even puts on her royal robes.

Down below, Sir Baron and Lady Casey sit discussing the latest developments of the war and whether or not the Queen is making a mistake. They both agree on the validity of the Queen's concerns about overstretching her army and economy, but both are hesitant to trust Dumelor. They cannot bring their concerns with him to Queen Korza, however, as they can't quite pinpoint why he's untrustworthy.

"It's just not good enough, Baron. His rise to power, however mysterious, is recognized as legitimate. Even so, if we knew he had taken power in Valendor through his own evil plot, which we cannot prove at all, I might add, it wouldn't matter. His forces are too few."

"I'm just so frustrated. The energy of the world is disturbed all around me. It must be from him."

"We are in a time of war, Baron. Perhaps this—" Lady Casey freezes. She looks around the room with fear and befuddlement in her eyes.

"Perhaps what?"

Ignoring the question, Casey says, "I feel as if a bucket of cold water has been dumped upon me, yet I am not wet. My breaths draw air, yet none fills my lungs... I have never felt this."

"Then you agree with me."

"Perhaps I do. Something is truly not right. I think we need to check on the Queen."

"But what will we say?"

"I don't know, but we need to make sure she is safe."

Baron follows Casey to Korza's chambers, but when they arrive, she is not there. Casey presses the guard on duty. "Where is the Queen?"

"She went to visit our guest, the Valendi Prince."

"What the blaze is she doing talking to him?" Baron asks.

"She did not say," the guard replies.

"Come on," Casey says to Baron.

They venture down through the fort to where Xastix is being held. When they finally arrive at the place, they find Korza in conversation with him. "Ah, Lady Casey and Sir Baron. Please welcome the newest member of the royal council." The Queen speaks as if she is dropping expected news.

Both Casey and Baron stare at her in disbelief. Finally, after a long pause, Baron musters up the courage to speak. "My Queen, apologies—I didn't quite hear clearly. Did you say the Valendi Prince, Xastix Dumelor, is joining the royal council?"

"Indeed. As the first Duke of Amoria, I am also delegating him the role of my top advisor. This role will continue throughout the war, and perhaps even after."

"What war?" Casey replies, still immensely shocked and confused.

"We will be joining forces with the Valendi and taking back what was stolen from us: the Freelands."

Casey and Baron still stand dumbfounded. Casey responds. "My Queen, that would be a violation of the Treaty of Belfhen. All of the northern kingdoms would likely declare war against us."

"Let them." Korza dismisses the concern. "Our combined forces will have more military might than them. Eventually, they will sue for peace."

"And what does the Valendi think about this?" Baron says, looking directly at Xastix.

Xastix finally speaks, breaking an intense stare he had been holding during the whole conversation. Beads of sweat trickle down his forehead.

"The Valendi have agreed to Korza's plan. And we will do this all to secure prominent representation in the new Amorian Empire. A new position of Duke shall be created that will be permanently occupied by a Valendi representative. That representative shall be me for now." He lets out a smile as he finishes his sentence.

Baron and Casey look at each other helplessly. "We will alert the others of your plans, my Queen," Casey finally says, bowing, after another contemplative pause. The two scurry off.

Xastix turns to Korza. "Come, let us discuss our next move."

"Of course. Follow me."

The two head to the main hall and discuss their future war for some time before General Medinus and Jof Dunharrow come bursting into the room. Ryder has a reserved demeanor, but Jof does not conceal his disgust at the Queen's change of heart. His stern voice carries off of the room's stone walls. "Queen Korza, I have known you since you were a child, and you have never made a decision, or done anything, rather, that made me stop and question your capacity to rule. I have always promised myself that I would tell you if you ever caused me to think this. Well, here we are, and I am telling you."

"You would question your Queen's ability to rule, Captain? If I didn't know any better, that would sound like treason," Korza sneers in response.

"My Queen, you are a good person. The New Baylands has never been stronger under your rule. Don't do this."

"I have heard enough. General Medinus, if we rally the army, can we take the Freelands?"

The General answers with as much confidence and composure as he can muster. "Possibly, but I am not sure it is worth the risk, or can be achieved without years of planning. We would likely be engaged by a combined force that could easily rival our own. The Aurelicans, Horventi, and Panorum would outnumber us alone, even without the help of the Ordish or Jyn. Plus, they would have the defensive advantage. The probability of launching a successful invasion out of thin air here, even with the help of the Valendi, would be low."

"Good. So, we do at least have the capacity to contend with all of them if we attacked?"

"I may—and I emphasize *may*—be able to get the army up to Aurelia City in the initial surge, but holding our lands will be near-impossible. Our eastern flanks would be heavily exposed and, with the army north, our own territory would be left undefended and vulnerable."

"Are you up for the task? Or should I ask a different general to lead the assault?"

"You know that if it is the will of the Queen, I will see it done."

"Good. Make preparations immediately. You will march the army back to Ezcbandia as soon as you are ready. We will gather our total strength there, and then you will drive the army north. You are both dismissed."

The two have turned and begun to walk away when the Queen stops them. "Wait. Jof, are you with me?"

"As long as I draw breath, I will protect you, Queen Korza. I have sworn to do so."

"Very well. You may go."

Jof and Ryder exit the room. As soon as they are out of sight and earshot, Jof immediately sets upon Ryder and pins him against the wall. "Have you lost your mind?" Jof asks aggressively.

"I would say the same to you," Ryder responds as he throws Jof off of him. "The Queen has given her commands, and we must follow."

Casey and Baron see the two men scuffling and run over to break it up. Jof, now being held back by Baron, says, "Never mind that this sudden change of plans is madness! The course of action we are taking is evil!"

"Taking back the Freelands, what is rightfully ours, is not evil. I understand our Queen's predicament. Our markets are at their breaking points. We need the resources, the farmland."

"Since when did you become an economist *and* a general? Can't you see? We are being deceived again by the Valendi. We will weaken our forces before they regroup and attack again!"

"Betray us with their Prince in our capital? I am not so sure about that."

Baron speaks up. "I agree with Jof—something is not right here. The Queen's decision is unlike her. And that goes without mentioning the energy disturbance around us."

"You can feel all you want, Knight, but I have orders that I must follow, regardless of my inclinations."

"Don't you understand?" Jof says in pleading anger. "We must all lobby her to change her mind. She will listen to all of us. You will march our army to its doom!"

"I will not jeopardize my career to question the Queen on this. I find your lack of confidence in me disheartening. The Valendi have proven themselves to be formidable opponents. They will be even stronger allies. If you all are so worried about our Queen, why don't you keep a close eye on her while I am gone?"

"You put your own personal gain in front of your responsibility to your kingdom!" Jof says derisively.

Ryder matches Jof's aggressive tone. "You are getting old, Jof. Your vision for the New Baylands lacks any ability to see past what you yourself will not reap. Now, if you will excuse me." He strides out of the room.

"What is becoming of this world?" Jof laments.

17

Under Fire and Mountain

Aris desperately throws snow off of him. He was initially buried a few feet down in an avalanche that followed the explosion, but now, with his head and shoulders above the surface, he looks around to evaluate the situation. The clouds have dissipated, and the morning sun has summited the mountains in the east, reflecting a bright light off of the snow-covered valley floor.

He looks back at the outpost to see Autoch lining the cliffside, firing on the valley below. Pockets of snow pop up as the gunfire narrowly misses him.

"Aris! Get to our position!" a voice yells from behind him.

It's Captain Ben. He has taken refuge behind a large boulder that must have rolled off the mountainside years ago. The rest of the survivors are scattered behind trees and boulders just off the slopes of Ilantum.

Aris finally frees himself and sprints to Ben's position while shots land inches from him. One bullet scrapes his side and rips his chainmail, but luckily, it's just a scratch. He slides next to Ben and grabs his injured stomach, letting out a grunt in frustration.

"Well, at least you still have your luck," Ben says reassuringly as he attempts to return fire over the boulder. "I guess you are not allowed to die while you are still responsible for protecting me."

Aris looks at what's left of the Eastfort garrison—some thirty-six men and women in total, made up of seventeen Panorum, seven Horventi, including Commander Azen, five Ordish, four Aurelicans, including Princess Skyler, one Jyn, and Aris himself, along with the Ithoran Inpyrian Jet Ikonobo. The survivors are all from Ben's makeshift squadron that had been pressed up against the edge of the cliff at the time of the explosion.

All the way back at the Ilantum Outpost, the Shadow Knight watches the last stand of the garrison through his spyglass. "Get those cannons turned around, and fired on the valley below," he commands in the Autoch tongue, referring to the cannons placed at the top of the ridge and meant to overlook the Orus Pass. "There are still high-value targets down there. We are not finished here until they are eliminated. And someone find a way down."

A Panorum soldier runs up next to Aris. "Have any extra rounds? I'm out."

Aris nods and hands him a clip. "Thanks, Freelander."

He loads his gun, and pops back up to return fire when a cannonball flies in and knocks his head right off. The cannonball smashes into the snow just behind Aris.

"Cannon-fire!" Princess Skyler yells.

Aris, now covered in the blood of the fallen soldier, hides in shock behind the boulder. Most of the cannonballs miss, but one drills a small rock where two Horventi are hiding. The debris from the rock's explosion rips through the two soldiers, killing them instantly.

"Take your ammo back from that soldier. He won't be needing it anymore," Ben says to Aris before sprinting over to the dead Horventi to do the same.

Aris reluctantly goes over to the Panorum body and pulls out the unused clip from his gun. Just seconds after he and Ben move, a cannonball strikes where they had been taking cover, smashing part of their boulder into smaller fragments. Aris abandons his position and runs back to where Commander Azen is stationed, while Captain Ben sprints to Skyler's cover.

Jet, who has found cover behind a tree with three Ordish, suddenly leaps out into the open without even looking, dodging a cannon ball that smashes right through the tree trunk and into one of the Ordish soldiers. The flying wood cuts right through another's throat, while the third is crushed as the rest of the tree falls to the ground.

Skyler, sweaty and exhausted, turns to Ben. "Captain, we can't stay here. We are cannon-fodder, and it's only a matter of time before the Autoch find their way down here."

Away from the Ilantum slopes, the valley is barren and provides no cover. The west valley is flanked by cliffs with a frozen waterfall in the center, while the east valley seems to have one gap that they may escape through in between the mountains.

Ben responds. "I agree. The east looks like the best way out, but it's the wrong direction. We should head north, summit the mountain, then break back westward. I am not sure it will be a traversable path, but it beats dying here."

Skyler nods.

"Make for the northern mountain now!" Ben yells out to the survivors.

Two Panorum soldiers near the back are the first to break out into the open valley. They are gunned down almost instantly by what must be at least fifty bullets. "Hold!" Azen yells after witnessing their evisceration.

The rest of the group retakes cover. "We have no choice, Captain. We must go east," Skyler implores him.

Captain Ben closes his eyes and sighs. This course of action will certainly inhibit their ability to warn Starlinden about the impending attack. "So be it. Let's go!"

The soldiers begin to run again. This path does have the cover of trees all the way out, but they only make it forty feet before they are stopped again.

"Oh, blast!" Ben says to himself as he spots several Autoch running toward them. They have found a way down.

"Take cover! Enemies advancing!" he yells.

Ben dives behind a fallen tree trunk. One Horventi and Ordish soldier ahead of him don't find cover in time, and are gunned down. Aris slides in behind the trunk next to Ben and rests his head against the bark to help catch his breath.

"Well Aris, I am afraid this is it. I am sorry I couldn't get you home. Let's let this be a noble end."

Aris, still breathing heavily, gives a stuttering reply with fear in his eyes. "It... it was an honor to serve you, Captain."

"Ben!" Jet yells as he sprints towards the two of them, parrying enemy gunfire with his sword. "We must head west. We can escape the valley there."

"West!? The valley is enclosed in the west."

Jet, now behind the trunk with them, responds. "It is the will of nature. I can't explain it, but I sense it."

"I trust you, Jet—maybe just because I don't have any better ideas. Lead the way."

"Follow me!" Jet commands to the rest.

The group once again breaks from cover and sprints west. Cannonballs and bullets continue to rain down from the mountain while their pursuers level shots at them. A Panorum soldier is felled when he is shot in the back, while a Horventi soldier running next to Azen is ripped apart by a cannonball that lands upon him.

Nevertheless, the group presses on.

It only takes a few minutes for them to near their target. "Look!" Jet exclaims. "Part of the waterfall has melted. There is space to go underneath."

Indeed, the morning spring sun has shaken the cold and snowy night that has preceded it, and the ice is melting. There is now a three-foot space between the frozen falls and the ground.

"Isn't there just a cliff behind it?" Ben asks.

"Let's hope not," Jet replies.

In order to the reach the waterfall, the last part of the run must be done in the open. The group becomes completely exposed, but they are now so far away from the outpost that the Autoch struggle to hit their mark.

Up on the mountain, an Autoch captain speaks to the Shadow Knight. "My lord, the enemy is all but out of range from us, save for our cannons."

"Save your bullets. They are trapped. Our ground force will soon wipe them out."

Jet is the first to reach the waterfall. He rolls underneath it over icy snow, then pokes his head back out to the others. "There is space behind it. Everyone underneath!"

One-by-one, the survivors crawl through.

The Shadow Knight discovers what is happening as he peers through his spyglass. "Concentrate all cannon fire on that waterfall!" he commands.

The last to make it to the waterfall are the Aurelicans with Princess Skyler. They are almost through when the cannon fire strikes the ice and cliff-wall above them. Loyal to the end, one of the Aurelicans shoves Princess Skyler through before she herself is crushed by the falling ice and rock.

From his vantage point, the Shadow Knight inspects the damage. A pile of shattered ice and stone now rests against the cliff wall. "Hold your fire!" he commands.

Izedar then speaks to himself in his native Amorian tongue. "That is the end of it. If any were not crushed, they will surely be trapped there. They have chosen their own tomb."

Now he addresses his force once again. "Rally up and get the soldiers below back up here. We will take the southern slopes of this mountain to rendezvous with the main force on the Orus Pass. And hurry up. We don't want to be late."

Down behind the waterfall, the last survivors come to grips with their predicament, as they now stand trapped in complete darkness.

Ny Azen breaks the silence. "Well, that maneuver bought us a few more hours before our inevitable deaths, although I am not sure I would have preferred to go out this way."

"Everyone remain calm. We must preserve oxygen if we are to maximize our chances of survival," Ben advises.

"Survive how, Captain?" Azen retorts.

"Quiet! I need to concentrate," Jet interjects.

The group's heavy breathing echoes off the cave walls. A few moments later, Jet speaks again. "There! It's here! This must have been what was calling to me."

Jet picks up a crystal covered in dirt from the ground and dusts it off to reveal a faint white light emanating from it that illuminates the area directly around him. The light makes him a beacon in the dark cave. "This crystal is carved. None are naturally shaped like this."

He turns back to the cave wall opposite from their entrance. "And this is not a natural cave wall."

He holds the light up to it, and the whole group can clearly see that the face is completely flat and perpendicular to the ground. The wall rises as far as the light can shine. There is only one blemish—a tiny gap bisects the wall from what seems like the top to the ground and intersects six feet above the dirt with a hole the same shape as the crystal.

"It must have fallen out somehow," Jet surmises. He places the crystal in the aperture, and its glow intensifies. Its light streams out right and left, drawing a column on each side before eventually reuniting atop the wall after scribbling something in unintelligible lettering.

Then, the cave wall opens.

18

The Mirage of Suportep

Sweat runs down Niike's forehead. The desert heat beams down upon him and envelops his army behind as it emanates from the dusted ground.

Sir Numenkor walks up next to him. "King Niike, the army is parched. Let us hold here and wait to advance in cooler temperatures."

"This dry heat is nothing compared to the humidity of the Ithoran Jungle. I will not stop. Not when I can see my prize."

Indeed, on the horizon, the oasis city of Suportep can be seen resting on and in front of the Blades, Amoria's southernmost mountain range. The city is situated at the southwest corner of the Senduine, the arid desert that takes up most of Zyber. Suportep is for the most part the one place in the desert where it actually rains, as every so often, storm clouds become pinned in the corner of the mountain range, causing massive flooding. Zyberian irrigation engineering allows control of the floods, thus giving the walled city the ability to grow crops, along with a grassy interior lined with palm trees growing next to its artificial rivers. This is why Suportep is referred to as Amoria's oasis city—it's a dot of flourishing life in the otherwise-barren desert.

Suportep is massive in total area. Half of it lays sprawled on the desert floor, while the other half intertwines itself in the brown rocky mountains it's adjacent to all the way west to the ocean. The city's architecture is uniform in its style, pulling from the resources of the region and the kingdom's major exports, with light-brown sandstone structures accentuated by dark-red clay tile roofs and iron doors.

The lower city is surrounded by walls on one side and mountains on the other. Its outer wall is shaped in the form of a trapezoid, connecting from western mountains to southern, and protects the city's crops and general buildings, which lie gridded together on the desert floor. On a normal spring day, most citizens tolerate the heat and either work their fields or peddle their wares at their local markets when they themselves are not going for a relaxing swim in one of the aqueducts.

The upper city is more spread out. Structures, varying from larger homes, administrative buildings, and mines, are dotted across the mountainside, only connected by narrow winding roads. The upper city is protected by a fifty-foot-wide irrigation channel, the Filec Aqueduct, that lines the base of the mountains.

Atop the tallest and cornermost mountain, dubbed Mount Kelutec by the Zyberians, lies the royal citadel. The flat plateau peak both allows for the citadel's immense size and gives it visibility over both the Senduine and the coast, where there is a port to facilitate any trade that wishes to circumnavigate the harsh desert.

The citadel is the gem of the Zyberian people. It's as much a garden as it is a government headquarters. Every building has plants and artificial waterfalls sprawling from its sides, and all of the buildings sit on the edge of the plateau, surrounding an inner garden containing a long and shallow pool in its center. The main building, where the Queen resides, sits at the northern edge of the plateau. The square building mirrors the architecture of the rest of the city, save for its height; it's five-stories tall, with the final story acting as the throne room. The room is three times the height of the rest of the stories, with a light-brown marble floor, and is surrounded by spread-out circular columns rather than an actual wall.

In the room, Queen Zila sits on her throne facing out to the Senduine, watching the Ithorans advance upon her home. The sandstone throne has four chairs facing in each direction like a compass. Zila is dressed in a royal white tunic with gold embroidery, which has turned more a cream color through years bathing in the sand. The tunic is the traditional garment of all Zyberians, and can be any color or sport any design. They are made of thin cloth and cover as little skin as possible so as to not trap heat. The Queen herself also wears a gold tiara, along with gold cuffs and a gold necklace with an ovular turquoise-glowing crystal set in its pendant.

The officially promoted Commander Alet Nesten approaches Zila. "Do not fear, Queen Zila. The city is more than prepared for the siege. We can outlast them for years, despite our current refugee population."

"That is exactly my fear, Commander Nesten. The Ithorans don't have the patience or the time to besiege us, meaning there is only one option: a full-scale assault of the city."

"Our walls are properly fortified, and our army is ready. If it comes to battle, we will repel the enemy."

Queen Zila looks back out to the sea of advancing soldiers. "Are you so certain, Alet?" she says concernedly. "I want lines of three stationed across the entire wall, and every cannon manned. Keep the majority of our army held behind in reserve to ambush any Ithorans who make it through. And have Lieutenant Zaltep rally what Inpyrians we have available in the city and distribute them amongst our force. Never before have their skills been so desperately needed."

"As you wish, my Queen."

"This is it, Commander. I don't have to inform you that there is nowhere left to run, and that there aren't any ships to whisk us all away to safety. Tell the army the same."

***

The Ithorans are now only a few miles away from their target. Niike gestures to Numenkor. "Have our legions encircle the capital, and make sure they stay out of range of the enemy cannons. Disperse our Knights at each of the three gates. Once each section is ready, tell them to light a torch. When every torch is lit, we march to our glory."

"Perhaps it would be wise to rest before we attack. We have been marching for days. The sun burns your forces, without a cloud in the sky to give them respite. Taking Suportep will be very difficult. It has only been done once in the history of Amoria."

"Every moment we delay gives our enemy more time to prepare and regroup. Do not forget that the Zyberian army, too, must have only just arrived a few days ago back at the city. If we can secure the lower city now, we can snuff out the rest of the capital via siege. The key to capturing Suportep is eliminating the crop supply that runs up against the outer walls. All it takes is one moment of weakness for the Zyberians to retreat and relinquish their outerposition, thus sealing their own fate."

"As you command, Niike. I will inform the other Knights and officers of the plan."

***

Zila now sees the Ithoran army fanning out, surrounding her capital. She stands alone in the shadow cast by the palace roof, staring out at the city still basking in the midday light. After several minutes, she finally breaks her gaze. "Kille, bring me my armor," she commands one of her servants.

The immense weight of her responsibility to save her kingdom presses down upon her like she is wearing an anvil on her back. Zyber has already suffered so much loss and defeat. Deep inside of her, she can feel herself buckling against the fate of her imminent future.

Kille returns and removes Zila's formal clothes to replace them with a nondescript cloth tunic. Methodically, the servant removes her jewelry, save for her necklace, and then dresses her in her metal royal armor.

All the while, Zila stares blankly forward, her mind lost in thought. A single tear runs down her right cheek.

Kille hands the Queen her sword and pistol. Zila wipes her tear, sheathes her sword, and holsters her gun. She turns away from her view and heads to her steed.

***

"King Niike, the torches are lit," Numenkor reports.

"Let the end... begin."

Numenkor makes a single gesture forward with his left arm, and the entire Ithoran army advances. Before they come into range of the enemy cannons, Niike turns around to address his army, marching backwards to keep pace. "Ithorans! Long have we lived in the shadow! Long have we been forgotten and forsaken! Long ago, we came to these lands; today, we finally establish our kingdom! For Ithora!"

Cannon fire rings out from the Suportep wall as he finishes, smashing into the front ranks of the Ithorans. Niike turns and charges at the wall, and the soldiers near him follow suit. Like a ripple, the rest of the army begins to break into a charge all the way to each end.

Once the Ithorans are in range of the Zyberian rifles, the Zyberians waste no time opening fire. More Ithorans are downed, but many are able to block the shots with their shields. There are far too many Ithorans for the Zyberians to take them all out. They reach the outer wall.

"Get the ladders up!" Niike yells, panting. Adrenaline courses through his veins and shades his mind from the heat.

Hundreds of ladders begin rising against the walls. The Ithorans' cannons, which they've plundered from the other Zyberian cities, are now in range as well, and begin to fire on the wall, despite endangering their own force.

The Zyberian walls are built of reinforced sandstone. It will take countless shots from the cannons for them to crumble. The iron gates, while also reinforced, are more vulnerable. It won't take as many hits to breach them.

Niike isn't going to put himself in the dangerous position of trying to take the wall with the rest of his soldiers. He makes for the city's central gate, hugging the face of the wall.

The first Ithorans to summit the wall are met with certain death, gunned or cut down almost instantly. However, their flow cannot be contained, and, in little time, there is ferocious hand-to-hand combat on the ramparts. Both sides are suffering heavy casualties, but the Ithorans bear the worst of it. With a large part of the Zyberian army held back, the Ithoran cannon barrage has been as deadly to their own force as their enemy's. The Zyberian defense on the wall is bending, but not breaking, with small reinforcements being dispatched to aid whenever Commander Nesten identifies a weak point.

Eventually, the inevitable happens: the city's central gate breaks from its hinges after relentless cannon-fire and falls inward to the ground. Numenkor leads the Ithoran charge into the farmlands that occupy the outer portions of the city. Niike is close behind.

Commander Nesten dispatches a third of the rest of the Zyberian force to meet them at the gate, including several camel cavalry regiments. The other two gates in the south and north also fall soon after, and Nesten dispatches similar-sized forces to meet the invaders.

The only force still remaining back is Queen Zila and her personal elite band of citadel guards, called the Sunstriders. A force of a hundred soldiers, the Sunstriders' first directives are to protect the city of Suportep and to defend the Queen. To be named a Sunstrider is a top honor for the average Zyberian foot-soldier. They wear standard Zyberian armor, save for their capes, which are sewn with vertical gold stripes, and their helmets, which are gold-winged, much like other Zyberians officers'. The Sunstriders' wings distinguish themselves from others by their style: three longitudinal stripes protruding from the same point on each eye-slit edge, growing from short on the bottom stripe to long on the top. Each Sunstrider is mounted atop a camel for this battle, and wields a rifle or sword in one hand and a triangular shield in the other.

The fighting at the gates is fierce. The Zyberians have had success defending the wall, but their ground defense is being put under much more pressure. The Ithorans are concentrating most of their forces on taking the three gates. If just one falls, the Zyberian defensive line will be broken, and the entire lower city could be compromised.

The Zyberians, fighting knowing that the fate of their kingdom depends on their success, are able to hold the enemy to a standstill at the northern and southern gates. The central gate defense, however, is faltering, for Niike has placed his best soldiers there to overwhelm the Zyberians. Sir Numenkor himself makes short work of the average Zyberian foot-soldier in his way.

Zila can see this unfolding. "Commander, stay here and keep watch on the battle. Pull the forces back if I fail to contain the enemy."

"My Queen, I could be a great aid to us on the battlefield, and we have already dispatched all of our Inpyrians. I fear for your safety. Let me go in your stead."

"Commander Nesten, you are a great warrior, but I am our people's leader. My presence in the field will uplift our entire force. I need you to be my commander, not my protector, today. If I should fall in battle, you will lead our people."

"May we never see the day, Zila."

Zila rallies the Sunstriders, and together, they gallop towards the central gate. Before any Ithorans can spot them coming, they split up and smash into the Ithoran flanks, riding over their enemies as if they were not even there and rejoining at the center. Now, the front Ithoran force, including Numenkor, is completely surrounded and cut-off from the rest of their army. The Sunstriders move in from behind to completely wipe out the detached group.

Niike has not been caught in this trap. Seeing the catastrophe about to befall his force, he once again orders in his secret weapon, Sir Exzar's jaguar cavalry, into battle. Within minutes, the force sprints through the central gate and pounces on the Sunstriders, quickly slicing through their lines and sowing chaos. The jaguars claw down both the camels and their riders and feast on their prey.

Exzar himself spots Queen Zila amongst the Sunstriders. Without hesitation, he makes his move to eliminate her. Zila sees him coming at the last moment, and dives off her steed, narrowly avoiding Exzar's jaguar's bite, but losing grip of her sword in the process. The jaguar crashes into her camel, knocking it to the ground and forcing Exzar off of his mount.

Zila hastily tries to get up and mount her steed, but the jaguar won't let her take his meal. Its jaws meet the camel's neck, snapping its spine with its vicious bite. "Kill her!" Exzar orders the beast after gathering himself from his fall.

The jaguar turns and leaps at Zila with its jaws wide open. Still on her knees, she pulls her pistol from her holster and frantically fires. The bullet flies into the jaguar's mouth, through its brain, and out its head. The corpse smashes into her, knocking her from her knees and putting her back flat on the ground.

Exzar grunts angrily and begins to charge the dazed Zila. She gets back to one knee and fires at him as he approaches. He comfortably blocks each shot with his sword as he closes upon her. Zila, without her sword, has no way of blocking Exzar's impending attack. Exzar swipes away Zila's gun from her left hand, spins, and begins a right-to-left blade strike, when, seemingly out of nowhere, Commander Nesten rides in and decapitates Exzar with one swift cleave of his sword. Exzar's now-headless body's momentum continues into Zila, once again knocking her to the ground.

Zila throws the mangled corpse off of her. "Close one," Nesten says as he dismounts and helps Zila back up.

"I told you to wait behind!" Zila responds, trying to act angered.

"I did. I waited before coming to help you."

"Well, now that you are here, we have a battle to win."

"My thoughts exactly, my Queen."

"Find the Ithoran general. I believe he is an Inpyrian. Take him out."

"It will be done."

Nesten breaks back into the chaos. Zila finds her sword on the ground, then moves to the top of her fallen steed to gain a vantage point over the battle. There, she spots King Niike fighting Sunstriders a few hundred feet ahead, and anger fills her body.

She breaks for him. Deftly weaving through the chaotic battle, it does not take long for her to reach Niike. By then, he has felled more of her force and gained even more ground.

Zila stands before the Ithoran ruler and commands his attention. "King Niike! I sentence you to death for your crimes against Zyber!"

Niike scoffs and fires shots at her with his pistol. Zila dodges the first and grabs a shield off the body of a dead Sunstrider to parry the others. Niike tosses his now-empty pistol to the side and charges her. The two smash into each other like two trains on the same track. Niike swiftly knocks Zila's borrowed shield away from her, and they clash swords.

Zila fights with a vicious style. Her fast-yet-heavy strikes force Niike onto the defensive. Her anger, however, also fills her reckless abandon. With Niike surviving the initial onslaught, he now performs his own methodical attacks, using Zila's style against her. Now, Zila is on the defensive and being forced backward. Desperate to stop her retreat, she frantically swings her sword from an overhead position at Niike. Niike sidesteps the strike and, in one fluid motion, swipes his sword horizontally at her. She sees the move occurring at the last second and promptly thrusts her hips backwards in an attempt to elude the blade. The sword misses most of its mark, but still manages to level a deep cut below Zila's breastplate and above her belt. She screams in agony, drops her sword, and buckles to the ground, her feet sliding out from underneath her in the thin sand. She throws her hands out to brace her fall, but is in too much pain to rise from her knees. Blood spills from her stomach onto the dry dirt beneath her.

"Let this be the last breath of Zyber," Niike says as he steps forward and raises his sword high enough to generate enough force to pierce her breastplate.

Zila desperately looks around her for anything to block his blow. Instead, she spots the pistol of a fallen Ithoran to her right. She lunges for it, grabs it, and spins on to her back in one motion as Niike begins to plunge his sword downward. She fires before he can finish his move. The bullet catches Niike square in the chest, ripping through his breastplate due to its proximity. He instantly drops his sword and doubles over. She tries to fire again as he falls, but the gun is empty.

Zila, with a rush of adrenaline and a heavy grimace, wastes no time in rising and grabbing her sword from the ground. Without hesitation, she is beginning to swing it at the fallen Niike when Nesten calls out to her. "Zila, watch out!"

Coming in from behind her is none other than Sir Numenkor. She turns just in time to block his surprise attack as he barrels into her, sending her back to the sand. Nesten, who has been in pursuit of the Ithoran Knight, quickly takes position in between Numenkor and Zila.

Numenkor, with his eyes fixed on Nesten, grabs Niike and pulls him up. He whispers to his King, "Niike, we need to get you out of here."

Niike nods, and the two slowly try to move away. Nesten is jumping to stop them when several Ithorans set upon him, halting him in his tracks.

Numenkor councils Niike while supporting his weight on his shoulder. "Our momentum has been stopped. Our forces are deadlocked throughout the battlefield. The northern and southern offenses rout."

Niike, bleeding and barely able to speak, musters his commands. "Then the battle is lost. We need to regroup. Issue a full retreat."

"Sir, I must inform you—we have sustained heavy losses. This could be our last attack."

"Just do it," Niike says, letting out a grunt.

Numenkor spreads word of the retreat, and the Ithorans pull back. Those who were on the walls or who had become separated from the main force during the battle for the gates are condemned to be left behind and killed.

As Numenkor speculated, it is a crushing defeat for the Ithorans. Over half of their force has been destroyed, while only a third of the Zyberians have fallen, and Suportep has only suffered minor damage.

Numenkor fears the truth that their war is over. It is unlikely that they will ever be able to take the city now.

The Ithorans recede into the desert.

19

Limited Power

"Well, Sir Jet, I am not sure I have ever been proven wrong so quickly," Ny Azen says as he steps through the open space that was an impassible cave wall just a few moments earlier. "And I have never been so happy to be proven wrong."

Directly in front of the Eastfort survivors are steep descending stairs illuminated faintly by bright red-light streams embedded in the cave walls. The lights are not singular; rather, they look as if someone has drawn veins into the cave with luminescent paint.

Everyone moves down the stairs except for Jet, who stands at the top concerned. "Jet, are you coming, or do you wish to die up there?" Ben asks.

"Something isn't right about this place. I feel suffocated, and it has nothing to do with the scarce air. I have never felt an energy presence so strong, save for at the Inpyrium itself. I have also never felt such evil."

"Well, I will admit the lighting doesn't exactly make the place look cheery, whether I can feel this energy or not. However, there is no point in wasting your time up there. The quicker we get out of here, the better."

"That is, if we get out of here."

"From being the most optimistic to the most pessimistic, despite the best possible luck we could have had. You must really not like it here."

"I really don't," Jet says tentatively as he begins to descend.

The front of the group reaches the bottom, where they find another door. "Blast. It's locked," one of the Panorum says.

"Have you tried pushing a little harder?" the last surviving Jyn from the garrison says.

Without giving the soldier a chance to respond, she breaks into a short sprint and lowers her shoulder as she smashes into the wooden door. The door breaks from its rusted hinges entirely and falls to the floor.

The group is thoroughly impressed by the move, especially Devden Skip, the last of the surviving Ordish, who sports a wide grin on his face. "Nice one," Ben says with a slight chuckle. "What's your name, Jyn?"

"Callathar Ejyn, but you can just call me Cal."

"Well, Cal, I am glad you are still with us."

"I haven't survived near forty winters in the Jynland Waste to die in a southern spring," the stalwart woman replies without even a hint of jest.

As this conversation unfolds, Ny Azen takes a few steps further forward. He doesn't make it far before something loose on the ground causes him to slip and fall. He flails helplessly to the ground, but finds a softer landing than he might have anticipated. "What the blaze is all over the floor?" Azen asks, confused.

Ben looks down in response. "This place must be very old. The dust at my feet is an inch thick," he surmises, kicking some of it off his shoe into the air.

Jet, now at the bottom of the stairs and weaving through the survivors to the front, interjects with an uneasy statement. "Not dust—ash."

"What?" Ny asks as he looks at his left hand, which is still covered in the dust from him bracing his fall. He then turns his eyes left to a horrifying sight. A foot away from him stands a human-like figure made of the same "dust" he had fallen into. The figure is frozen in a running motion towards the door they had just broken through, with its mouth wide open, as if it had been trying to scream.

"Ugh!" Azen exclaims in disgust as he tries to wipe off his hands while rapidly backing away from the figure.

He takes only a few reckless steps backwards before he smashes into another. As soon as he hits it, he spins around in panic, just to find it falling apart upon him as if it were a dry sandcastle losing its form. Azen backs into the group, dusting himself off feverishly.

Looking forward, the group can see hundreds of these statue-like objects down the hall. The figures have similar statures to Amorians, with two arms and legs, one head, etc., but also some key differences—they have small wings protruding from their backs, what looks like fins jutting from their calves and spines, and gills on their cheeks.

"This is a cursed place," Ben says. "What are these things?"

"More like, what *were* they?" Jet responds. "The text above the entrance—it was in the Ancient's lettering. This would lead me to believe that we are the first Amorians to see what the Ancients really looked like. I know of no power that could do this on its own. It's more likely these are statues erected to commemorate some event here."

"Well, I don't know about y'all, but I would have gone for something less terrifying in remembrance," Skip remarks.

"The light emanating in this place could only be generated by a crystal of great magnitude," Jet says. "If we wish to find our way out of this place, I feel we must find the light's source."

The group continues cautiously through the hallway. Aris, in the middle of the pack, wonders to himself if this nightmare will ever be over. His fear and shock from his prior experiences is consuming him to the point that he struggles to think at all, and the haunting red darkness that surrounds him sinks his heart further. He moves slower than the rest of the group until he falls all the way to the back.

"Aris, is it?" a voice says to him.

He turns to see Princess Skyler looking directly at him. He snaps out of his trance to muster a response. "Y-yes... I am Ariscles Shanis of Baywood."

"Pleasure to formally meet you, Aris. I am Skyler Aurelia of Aurelica. You can call me Sky."

Aris obviously knows who she is, but it is a nice gesture by the Princess. The two grab the other's forearms as a customary greeting. Skyler reassures him. "In trying times like these, it is important that we stick together and remain sharply focused on the task at hand. We all depend on each other for survival."

The weariness on her face is undeniable, despite her efforts to hide it, but that only makes her words more powerful. They're all going through this traumatic experience and, to escape it, they will have to be stronger than they've ever imagined, but at least they will not be alone doing so. Aris retakes his normal pace and falls in front of Skyler in the group's line.

Discussion is limited as the harrowing journey continues. The ash surrounding them muffles them, making everything so quiet that their very own thoughts might as well be heard by each other. Tired and unnerved, the group passes by several other ominous hallways and doors with growing unsureness. "How do we know we aren't supposed to turn?" Azen asks Jet.

"Well, we don't. We must trust our intuition. There does appear to be a light at the end of the tunnel ahead." Indeed, far ahead of the group, the red light shines brightest. "I suspect we should follow the light."

When the group reaches the end of the hallway, Jet's suspicions are confirmed. They all step out onto a massive balcony, overlooking miles of stone-carved buildings and city streets, all illuminated by red veins of light in the cavern's endless ceiling, which now is hundreds of feet above their heads. On the edges of the cave, one can just make out waterfalls protruding from the walls, flowing down into steaming lakes throughout the city. The overall heat of the entire chasm is palpable, like stepping into an oven.

"A sight I shall not soon forget," Ben says in awe as he takes in the view.

"It's a blasted Ancient city!" Skip follows in wonder.

The buildings below are a controlled chaos of prisms, as if one took a box of the three-dimensional shapes and arranged them all the floor with spaces between each to ensure none would touch. Some buildings are as high as twenty stories, while many also are just one.

"We know the Ancients built mines, but an underground city? This is beyond our comprehension," Jet comments. "Although, interestingly enough, this place looks nothing like the Inpyrium." While the hallway they've come from had many ash statues lining its walls, it does not compare to the streets of the city below, which are packed with them to the point that it looks as if there is little to no space even to move in between them.

Jet now takes his eyes from the city below to the ceiling. "Look! The veins' light appears stronger over there. It must be near the power source," he announces, pointing to the other side of the ruins.

"I guess that means we have to cross the city," Ben replies.

Jet nods, and the group moves down the wide stairs protruding from the right side of the balcony. With their path now better lit, the group can see that the stairs lead all the way to the streets.

Although inefficient, navigating the city is easy. The only real issue is avoiding the statues, which many in the group incidentally bump as they attempt to weave through them. The result is identical as to when Azen fell back into the statue at the beginning of the cave—they instantly dissipate into the ground around them.

"These statues are different than the ones in the hallway," Jet states as the group makes their way through the city.

"They look just as horrifying to me," a Panorum soldier by the name of Eder says. "And they crumble all the same."

"They're armed," Ben states. "And they don't look fearful—they look angry. They're fighting each other!" he exclaims.

Indeed, the Ancient statues grip swords, shields, and bows in their hands, and appear to be depicted in armor. "Perhaps a great battle was fought here long ago, and these ash statues were erected to commemorate it as a sort of memorial," Azen posits.

"We know the Ancients were very powerful, but the detail at this scale is almost too good, even for them," Jet responds. "The further we move through this place, the more I question the fate of it."

The group continues until they finally reach what they are searching for at the other end of the city—a massive closed door lit brightly by the strong red lights above it. Everyone in the group is now damp with sweat. With the increase in light, there is also an increase in heat.

"We just keep getting lucky today," Azen says. "A nice change of pace from the few days prior, to say the least."

Azen's upbeat mood is due to the fact that, ahead of the group, a substantial hole has been punched through the closed wooden doors. It's at least twenty feet high and a hundred feet wide; compared to the doors themselves, which must stand 300 feet tall and a hundred feet wide each. The survivors move through the gap.

Through the doors is a steep and wide staircase that seems to climb as high as the ceiling of the city itself. "Our power-source must lie up there," Jet claims, pointing at a bright-red glow at the top of the stairs.

"Maybe I spoke too soon," Azen says, looking at the massive climb ahead of him, which is covered with more statues.

The group presses on. It takes some time for the weary survivors to make it up the towering steps. When they do, they finally find their answer for how the city is lit.

A grand circular cave surrounds a colossal bright red crystal in its center. The crystal roughly resembles the shape of a diamond, with what must be a seventy-foot vertical crack that stretches from its top point to its bottom. The light in the room is as if a setting sun rested in its center.

Jet is forced to look away, feeling great pain and suffering emanating from the crystal itself. "There is no crystal even close to the size of this one in Inpyrian records," he says.

"Can we use it?" Ben asks.

"Its energy—it's unlike anything I have ever felt before. It's overwhelming. Perhaps if I get close enough, I can uncover its power."

"Well, I am afraid you are going to have to knock a few of these over to do so," Azen says.

There is no longer space to move in between statues. The room is packed tight with them, and they're seemingly frozen in combat like those below.

Jet nods, draws his sword to knock the ash statues down and out of his way, and moves forward, keeping his eyes off of the crystal itself. The rest of the group follows in single-file behind him. At the base of the crystal, there is space of around twenty feet on all sides, with thicker ash covering the ground.

Jet has walked all the way up to the imposing crystal when he steps on what sounds like glass. Under his foot are shards of a crystal, only no light glows from them, for the crystal has been destroyed. He looks to his right to find a weapon that, at last, is not made of ash like the rest. It is a shimmering-yet-black obsidian staff, cracked into two pieces. At its end, there is clearly a place for a crystal to be set in it. "Perhaps this crystal used to belong to this staff," Jet hypothesizes.

"This crystal, its power—it's enthralling," the Panorum soldier Eder says, his eyes fixed on it. He has followed Jet forward.

"Wait, don't—" Jet exclaims as Eder reaches out to touch it.

It's too late. All it takes is Eder's pointer finger making contact with the crystal for it to react. A current of energy rips through it, brightening it immensely and momentarily blinding the entire group. Everyone shields their eyes and looks away. With a whirring sound like every key on a piano being played at once in a deep cavern, the current moves down into Eder, eventually hitting the cave floor and causing an explosion of force and red-lightning. The strength of the blast knocks the whole group from their feet and washes away the rest of the ash statues in the room.

Shaken, Ben looks back up at the crystal while slowly getting back to his feet. The energy spike is over. The crystal now glows as it did before. "This isn't a city. It's a mausoleum," he says in dread.

Standing next to the crystal is Eder, petrified in ash in the exact position he was as he made contact with the crystal.

Princess Skyler screams, aghast, causing all heads to turn her direction. One of the Aurelicans with her has also been struck by the lightning, and remains frozen in place. With a look of terror on her face, the Aurelican had raised her hands in front of her in a futile attempt to protect herself. Two other Panorum soldiers also have suffered the same fate.

"What horror is this!?" Azen asks rhetorically.

Jet laments, "It is as I feared. We cannot use the crystal. It has been corrupted."

20

A Dissemination of Strength

Smog fills the air above Ezebandia. The sun struggles to penetrate the artificial clouds overhead, trapping its heat and giving the Baylander capital an unnatural brown light.

Korza has ordered the city's factories into overdrive to prepare for the war. Day and night, armor is being crafted, weapons are being produced, and ships are being built. The kingdom's economy is stressed to its furthest, like a long piece of twine being stretched to its limits; one more pull, and it's bound to snap.

Ryder finds himself in familiar territory. He stands in his apartment in the royal palace, staying inside to avoid inhaling the fumes. He is under orders by the Queen to get some rest, but he is hardly able. He paces back and forth, fearing what's ahead and what is already transpiring.

Ryder lives on the tenth floor of the northwest building. His windows face outward, giving him a partial view of the western city, Olovor Bay, and the Rolling Hills, which surround Ezebandia. Every now and then, he glances outside to look at the entire Baylander fleet anchored in the bay. The sight does inspire some confidence, for it is the largest fleet in all of Amoria, large enough to inspire fear across all of the ocean coast, but he knows those ships can't fight his battles for him.

Ryder's anxiousness overwhelms him, and he swings open his apartment door, turns left down his hallway, and descends a stairwell to the bottom floor. He braves the smoky outdoors for a moment to cross the grassy courtyard before turning into the main building and ascending its stairs to his destination.

Ryder storms into the throne room unannounced, or so he thinks. The entire military arm of the royal council is there, along with the King. Admiral Walsh, Captain Dunharrow, Sir Baron, Lady Casey, Sir Edward, and Lady Daphne sit on wooden chairs facing the throne. Xastix sits in Captain Dunharrow's former chair to the right of the throne, the old and fat King Rodrick sits to its left, and Korza sits upon it.

"General Medinus." Korza speaks loudly to carry her voice clearly to the entryway. "I thought I ordered you to get some rest."

"Apologies, my Queen. I cannot be at ease with so much at stake."

"I can't say I am surprised. I left you an open chair just in case." She gestures to a seat in the middle of the group facing her. As Ryder walks over to sit, he can discern an uneasiness on the faces of his fellow advisors, especially Captain Dunharrow.

"Out of respect for the General, I was planning on withholding this announcement until tomorrow, but since Ryder is now here, I might as well give the full report." Korza looks over to Xastix, and he nods in approval. "Tomorrow, at midday, our army and fleet will launch from Ezebandia and make for the southern Freelands border. As you've likely assumed, Ryder will command our ground force, and Kent will command the fleet."

Korza focuses her eyes on Admiral Kent Walsh. "Admiral, do not outpace our ground forces. We cannot have the enemy move in behind our lines by sea."

"Of course, my Queen."

"Good. Lady Daphne will sail with you as an advisor and protector. The rest of the Knights on this council will join General Medinus. I expect you all to fight valiantly for your kingdom. Captain Dunharrow, Xastix, and King Rodrick will remain here with me at the capital."

Ryder is confused by her last sentence. "Queen Korza, if Xastix is to remain here, who shall command the Valendi army in battle? Which, by the way, has not even arrived at the city yet. I am not sure I can maintain sufficient command over an entire foreign force, along with my own."

"A valid concern, General. There has been a slight change of plan. Given the current geopolitical situation and my confidence in our military strength, Xastix and I have agreed that it is best the Valendi army be sent south to end the Zyberian-Ithoran war in our new allies' favor."

Ryder can feel a pit forming in his stomach. "Korza, as you know, our invasion of the Freelands is not simply a war against an army-less, un-unified people. It is a war against the five northern kingdoms. I will need every sword, gun, and cannon we can muster to succeed."

"Such lack of faith, General. Do you not see the city working tirelessly to reinforce you?" Korza laments mockingly. "And here I thought you were one of the few people I could count on for support."

"My Queen, I assure you, my wishes for victory do not differ from yours."

"Yet you lack proper clairvoyance. Your fear betrays you and threatens our entire purpose. Xastix warned me such would occur. I will refocus it." Korza now stares directly into Ryder's eyes with as much austerity that she can muster. "You will leave Ezebandia with our armies tomorrow, and I decree that you and your fellow Knights here will not return until you have captured and secured Aurelia City, under penalty of torture and death."

The entire room, save for Xastix, is stunned silent. The council members glance at each other with eyes begging whomever they meet to speak up and say something. Ryder tries to speak, but no words escape his mouth. He can feel his whole body shaking.

Aurelia City has never fallen in the history of Amoria.

After letting her order sit with the council members for a few seconds, Korza resumes in an even more forceful tone. "The time of the New Baylands is over. The age of the Amorian Empire has begun."

21

Implacable

It's midday in Starlinden, but one can hardly tell. An unrelenting fog has engulfed the city, giving the mountain city an eerie feeling.

Starlinden is really more of a province than a city. It encircles the entire west and southern bank of the Shimmering Sea, one of the largest lakes in all of the Amorian kingdoms. Its buildings are more like compounds; each one is spread out amongst the region's native pine trees, with multiple acres to themselves. The number of buildings in each compound varies, but the materials used remain the same. Stone, Panorus's top export, is used for the structures' foundations and walls, while wood is used for roofing. Compounds contain anywhere from three to twenty buildings, and have small farms in order to provide agricultural self-sufficiency. The larger compounds often have their own windmills and sawmills.

Panorus's economy is mostly supported by its mines, and Starlinden is the best example. The largest mine in the known world is built directly into the northernmost mountain in the city, Mount Lume. Named the Sky Mine due to the glowing white crystal-flakes that line its caves like stars, the mine has been a huge boon of wealth for the Panorum due to its reinforced stone, iron, and even gold content.

Perhaps this is why the capital building is built outside the entrance to the mine on the slopes on Mount Lume. The stone building is five stories high, built half-in and half-out of the mountain, with each lower floor protruding farther forward and asymmetrically wider as the mountain slopes outward. Each floor has its own flat wooden roof that the floor above uses as a deck. Stone archways on each floor give space for impressive glass windows that, on a clear day, provide a view of the entire city and its mountainous surroundings.

King Thandus Vodner has left the capital building today for some isolated relaxation and hangover recovery, something he can certainly use at his advanced age. He doesn't mind the mist; it makes him feel calm and away from his tribulations.

He uses today's free time to take out his personal rowboat onto the Shimmering Sea. Once satisfyingly distanced from the shore and with his modest fishing rod cast, he lies in peace, letting his hand drift into the water and brush up against the diminutive crystal flakes that give the lake its name when the sun shines down upon it.

Ruling Panorus is relatively easy compared to the tasks of some of the other leaders. The kingdom's position in the mountains makes it nearly impossible to invade, and its wealth is only rivaled by Aurelica and the New Baylands, whose populations are much greater. From time to time, King Thandus has to settle a dispute between compounds or deliver a reassuring speech after a mining accident, but otherwise, he spends his time like most

Panorum—partaking in outdoor activities during the day and enjoying hearty and beer-heavy meals at night.

Several hours pass while Vodner's mind wanders. He tries to focus his thoughts on only pleasant memories and optimistic futures, but can't quite keep a serene mind. Then he realizes it. "I haven't gotten a single bite on my line!" he says incredulously.

His annoyance snaps him completely out of his stupor. He can't even remember the last time he caught nothing. "Stupid smart fish," he sneers as he begins to row back to his home on the lakeshore, annoyed at his failure.

Thandus has smartly kept his boat tied to the dock with a long rope, as the mist has not evaporated with morning's maturity. As he follows it, it doesn't take many strokes for him to begin to hear a lot of gunshots ringing out from land.

"Have some blasted respect; it's still mid-morning," he mutters.

The King gets even closer, and now, he can hear yelling.

"Watch your left!"

"They're behind the trees!"

"Fall back!"

A cannon shot rings out. The booming noise turns Vodner from irritated to irate. "What the blaze are these barbarian brutes going off about now?"

What was supposed to be a quiet day is now going to be a day in which he settles another frivolous compound dispute. He takes his frustration out on his oars, rowing faster and harder to shore. At this new heightened pace, it doesn't take long for him to reach his dock. He hops out of his rowboat and ties it to the pier with fervor, muttering more obscenities to himself.

When he turns to walk off the dock, he stops in his tracks. Walking towards him is the fully-armored Shadow Knight. "Your guards mentioned this is where I might find you," Izedar says calmly.

"Idiots. Letting an armed man approach me unprotected. I will have to find new ones. Who the blaze are you, anyways?" Thandus replies with asperity.

The Shadow Knight reaches the King and answers menacingly. "Your doom."

Izedar swiftly draws his sword and plunges it through King Thandus's chest. Vodner looks down at his impaled sternum, then back up at Izedar. Shock is the only expression on his face now.

Izedar swiftly slides the blade back out of him and pushes him off the dock. The King lands in the lake face-down and floats back up to the surface in a pool of blood. Izedar leaves him either to drown or die from his wounds, whichever is quicker. He then walks off the dock and around the base of Vodner's two-story lake house, fading back into the mist.

22

A Shadow in Dying Light

"So, what do we do now?" Ny Azen asks. His question isn't directed toward anyone in particular, but rather, anyone who can come up with an idea.

"Our only path remaining is forward," Ben states with feigned confidence. He gestures to a hallway entrance at the end of the room, directly across from where they entered, and moves toward it. The others follow with unsureness in their steps.

"Are you coming, Jet?" Azen sees Jet has remained fixed in place, his head tilted towards the ground.

"The evil that lingers in the aura here is one that I have never encountered—such fear, hatred, and death, and yet such power." He turns to look at Azen. "If we spend much more time down here, I fear we shall be forever bound to its malevolence." He moves to join the rest, still shielding his eyes from the crystal.

A look of defeat covers the faces of the survivors now. One adversity after another has brought them past their breaking point. They are becoming resigned to their fate: death.

Skyler has taken the latest turn of events the worst. Only moments before, she had remained one of the last calm and collected members of the group, feeling it was her responsibility as a leader and as a member of the Aurelican royal family to maintain a look of poise and confidence. Now, her heart has finally given in. She follows at the back of the group so as to not be seen with tears running down her cheeks, trying her best to contain her trembling. Her training at Ostis has not prepared her for this.

***

This hallway goes on for what seems like miles, with petrified Ancients still providing an obstacle course. Every fifty or so odd feet, the group passes by another connecting hallway and wonders if they are missing their escape route.

"I reckon we should split up," Devden Skip posits.

"No. The only thing that awaits us down those paths is nothingness," Jet warns.

"Are you sure?"

"No."

This answer doesn't exactly give Skip a boost in morale. "Then how can you be sure nothingness doesn't await down this path as well?" he asks with rhetorical annoyance.

Ben interrupts. "Our fate may yet still be the same, but there is budding hope. Look at the cave walls. The red glow is fading, yet far ahead of us, there remains light."

Deep in the distance, the hallway appears to end, and a brighter light illuminates it. As the group approaches it, it becomes clear that it isn't the same red light that fills the Ancient city's halls, but a purple light that filters through archaic wooden doors.

When the group reaches them, Ben tries to push through the doors, but they just crumble into dust. "Whoops," he says flippantly in an attempt to lighten the mood. His humor falls flat.

The disintegration of the doors reveals a massive room, shaped to resemble an auditorium facing the right wall, with at least twenty rows of carved seating. The entire left wall and ceiling is made of transparent crystal. Behind it, there looks to be a body of water with glittering flakes floating in it, giving the room a blue light that counteracts its red glow.

"The Shimmering Sea!" Ben exclaims in excitement. "Could it really be it?!"

"Over here!" Azen says as he breaks into a slight jog toward the right side of the room.

Lining the entire right wall is what looks like a map of the entire city. The complexity of the drawing is overwhelming, save for a bright white star that is drawn at its left-center.

"This has to be where we entered," Azen says, pointing at the rightmost feature of the map. He then runs all the way over to the left. "Perhaps this is our exit." He now gestures to a blue triangular-shaped room that runs up against the wall. His eyes race back and forth, studying the map. "We must be here. We aren't far!" he says, pointing at the only half-circle in the entire painting.

Morale in the room is noticeably improving for everyone except Sir Jet, who has largely ignored Azen due to his fixation on an old book lying on the floor. "This book is of our design," he expresses with curious wonder.

Hardly anyone hears him; their gazes instead fixated on the map. Jet walks over, picks up the book, and dusts off the cover. "An Inpyrian journal!" he exclaims louder.

Now, he has the room's attention. He examines the book's leather cover with Inpyrian markings along with its vellum pages. Its particular style indicates it's over 500 years old. He opens up the book to find a name on the first page, along with a date. He reads aloud. "Lady Elafyre Valenor, twenty-five years since the Annihilation."

He looks up with an expression of bewilderment. "Impossible..."

"I am not sure what's more astounding: that Amorians have been here before, or the last name," Ben responds.

"Well, whoever this was didn't get a chance to report her findings. There are no records of this place in the Inpyrium Archives. Perhaps she received the same fate as the Ancients here." Jet closes the journal and tucks it against his chest. "I am taking this back to the Inpyrium. This mystery can be unraveled there, when we aren't as pressed for time."

Ben nods and then gives his order. "Commander Azen, lead the way." He then addresses the group as a whole. "Let's get out of here."

Azen charges up the stairs that he believes lead to the exit. The entire group's energy is reinvigorated. They move with pace and purpose. Aris, retaking his position beside Ben, asks him a question. "Valenor—is that the last name of the kings of the old world?"

Ben replies, "Indeed, it is. The Valenor family ruled the old world Valendor for as long as written history, helping guide their kingdom to unmatched splendor."

"I thought they were all killed in the Annihilation?"

"According to the history books, they were. The line was ended across the ocean, officially marking the end of unequaled Valendi power in both the old world and the new. If the Inpyrian visitor here was, in fact, a Valenor, she must have not lasted long after. It's even possible she faded into obscurity, as only kings can rule Valendor."

The stairs wind and are certainly steep, but eventually, Azen reaches the top. In front of him stands an opening as high as the one they entered through, though this gate is lit by bright red light-stream columns on its side, and has no door. Azen walks through the opening to find the triangular room he was searching for, with him at its apex. "Blast!" he cries in frustration.

In front of him are steps that descend directly into a steaming lake that fills the rest of the room. Even the red lights flow down into it. Jet looks for an exit in the walls or ceiling, but he finds no options on the walls, and can't see far enough through the dark even to make out a ceiling.

"The energy of the crystal lights flows down, carries past the back wall, and then fades. I sense nothing after," Jet says.

"Perhaps we should go back to the map and search for another potential escape," Skyler suggests.

"Every second we lay trapped down here is another second lost to the Autoch marching on Starlinden," Ben replies with conviction in his tone. "I'm not leaving here until we are certain there isn't an exit."

He unties his green cloak and removes his chainmail armor. Then he puts his cloak back on and, without giving anyone a chance to question or protest, dives into the lake.

The water is very warm, for it's heated by the crystal-streams, all of which flow downward to a cylindrical opening at the bottom of the submerged stairs and encircle it. Ben swims through the short twenty-foot-long tube and out its other side, which isn't lit.

Minutes pass while the group waits behind. With each passing second, worry grows and hope fades, but the group remains. Then, just as the group begins to assume the Captain's death, five minutes after he initially submerged himself, Ben emerges. "Take off your armor. We are home," he states triumphantly while treading water.

"What did you find!?" Azen asks with enthusiastic curiosity.

"The liquid pathway leads into a natural cave—only this cave has already been discovered by our people. It's part of the Sky Mine. We are underneath Mount Lume!"

Hearing this, everyone hurriedly doffs their heavy armor to prepare to swim to freedom. Jet, capable of swimming in his leather armor, spends his time lamenting the fact that he will have to leave Elafyre's journal behind, as the ink would surely be ruined in the water. *Perhaps this is why it was left here in the first place*, he wonders to himself as he sets it down.

"Shall we?" Ben asks.

The group dives in. One by one, everyone makes the short swim through the cylinder and surfaces on the other side. From there, they swim over to the underground lake's stone shore, with the water turning colder with every stroke further.

Once ashore, Aris stares in awe at the cave they have entered. "So, the legends are true. An underground night-sky."

"Indeed, Aris," Ben responds proudly. "To the Panorum, this is the most beautiful sight in the world."

"I only wish my friend Epi could have seen this. He always claimed it was a merchant's myth."

"There is always a bit of truth in myths."

Azen looks around the cave. Pickaxes and tracks for mining carts lay scattered in the vast cavern. "Captain Ben, where are we?"

"The Myki Cavern—the lower levels of the Sky Mine, and just about a half a mile from the mine's entrance."

"Shouldn't there be miners?"

Ben freezes, coming to a slow realization. "There should. We could be too late. We must hurry. Come on!"

The dripping-wet and fatigued group breaks into a jog to follow Ben through winding caves and up some makeshift stairs, dodging minecarts and tools left scattered and unorganized. Their pace allows them to reach the mine's only entrance and exit quickly—a series of three archways carved into Mount Lume's vertical slope, aligned next to each other. The two archways on the outside are roughly a hundred feet tall and fifty feet wide, while the central archway is 400 feet tall and 200 feet wide. From the inside, one can only see the cylindrical columns supporting each of these archways, lined backwards in rows to support the carved entrance's interior. Stone flooring covers the ground of the entrance grotto, leading all the way out to wide stairs that spill onto Mount Lume's slopes like a waterfall flowing into a forest.

Ben sprints past the entrance and to the edge of the stairs now basking in the evening's last orange light. His eyes still need time to adjust, but the picture of the vast forested city is clear. The very mist that also covered the Eastfort now lingers in east Starlinden, and fires are scattered across the city itself. Burning compounds litter the south bank of the Shimmering Sea. Gun and cannon-fire ring out from the forest, muffling indecipherable screams.

The rest of the survivors join Ben at the edge of the stairs. "So, we are too late," Azen laments. "It is as you feared, Captain."

"Too late to provide warning, but not too late to save my people," Ben responds with shaken resolve. "Just down the slope to the southeast is the capital building. We can rendezvous with King Thandus there and ascertain the severity of the situation. We have many troops stationed here in the city, both active and inactive. An Autoch force cannot simply walk in here and claim our capital. Follow me."

The non-Panorum survivors throw concerned glances around to each other, as if each is questioning with their eyes whether they should still stay with Ben. For lack of a better idea, they reluctantly follow. Of the total group of Eastfort survivors, only nineteen remain, with ten of them being Panorum.

The entrance to the capital building from the north is built directly into its top roof, a simple stairway leading down into the structure's top-floor main hallway. Upon reaching it, Ben strides down the steps with haste, and his soldiers follow tightly behind. Just as he enters the hallway, a bullet whizzes past him and into the chest of a Panorum soldier to his right, knocking the soldier down. "Take cover!" Ben yells.

The entire group dives behind the little coverage the hallway's columned archways provide. Down the hall, Autoch forces lay fire upon them. Another Panorum is downed. Skip, being a member of Captain Liber's former sniper team, uses his rifle to gun down four Autoch in quick succession. Jet moves from his back column to lead the push forward, parrying shots away as they are levied upon him, and Ben immediately moves behind him, giving the rest of the group the courage to do the same. They charge down the hall, gunning down more Autoch in the process. Eventually, they are in melee range of the last of their enemies. Led by Jet, they cut them down by sword with ease.

The end of the hall leads into a vast room. On the north side is a fifteen-row grandstand. On the south side is a long wooden table, with seats placed only facing the stands. Behind the table is a wall covered completely in glass with sweeping views of Starlinden. Now, the table has been flipped to its side, with Panorum soldiers firing from its cover. From the stands, Autoch rain gunfire on the Panorum.

Ben and company enter the room behind the Autoch, and before the Autoch can even react, the group is upon them. They are cut and gunned down with ease.

With the fighting abated for now, a man rises from behind the table, using the table's edge to support himself. However, this is not the man Ben expects to find. "General Fonder!" Ben says concernedly, rushing to him.

He is wounded. Gunshots have entered both his hip and left shoulder. "Captain Ben," Fonder says weakly. "You survived."

"Hardly, General." Ben puts his right arm on Fonder's side to support him. "We were all-but wiped out."

Fonder puts his right arm on Ben's shoulder and squeezes tightly. "Unfortunately, the same can be said here." Ben's concerned look in response to this news is unquestionable. "They are too many."

Fonder's grip fails, and he slumps toward the ground, only held up by Ben's right arm. Ben gently allows him to lay down and hurdles the table. "We need to get you treated for these wounds, General."

"No!" Fonder says sharply, followed by muffled coughing. "It is over. Our remaining forces are depleting as we speak, and King Thandus, along with the rest of the royal family, is surely dead."

"How do you know this?"

"The family was at the royal estate when the city was attacked. It now burns. Our armies pushed to retake the position, but we were repelled before we could even come close."

"Where can I find the rest of the army?"

"The city is lost!" Fonder coughs blood and grabs Ben's shirt with his left hand. "Listen to me, Captain. Go to the stables, commandeer a horse, and leave this place, for if you stay, it shall be your grave. As it is mi..." He doesn't get the chance to finish his last sentence before the life fades from his eyes.

Ben slowly stands above his lifeless body, then looks out to the burning city behind him. He lets out a deep sigh, then turns to the group. "We must make for the stables and leave this place. My home now lies under the embers of the enemy."

***

The Eastfort survivors, now joined by an additional five Panorum who were with Fonder, burst out from the bottom floor of the capital building and run towards the stables in the southwest corner of the city. A long, two-story wooden barn, the Starlinden Stables can house over 500 horses at a time.

Unfortunately, they only make it a few hundred feet through the forested lower slopes of Mount Lume before being engaged by Autoch. The survivors dive behind trees and boulders for cover—that is, except for Jet.

"There is no time to hide!" he yells out to the group. "The longer we wait, the more our window of escape slips away from us!"

Skyler, with great reluctance, spins from behind a tree and keeps moving. Azen and Ben do the same. The rest follow suit.

The group continues to move toward its target, but not without casualties. A surviving Horventi soldier is dropped by Autoch fire, along with four Panorum. It is truly a frantic run through the trees. Aris sees shots land next to him and smash against trees beside him every ten feet. Even a slip guarantees one's death, for the group is not waiting for its wounded or stragglers.

Several Autoch rush the survivors to engage in them in hand-to-hand combat, and while many experienced fighters like Azen, Ben, and Jet shake off their attackers with relative ease, others are overwhelmed and felled. Their desperate cries are haunting, but, nevertheless, they must be left behind.

Aris is luckily positioned well in the mad dash. The non-Panorum survivors have stuck together as followers, as they do not even know which direction the stable is. This positions Aris amongst most of the group's best warriors, and whenever an Autoch reaches them, there are always multiple fighters available to dispatch the enemy.

By the time the group finally reaches the stables, the Panorum have suffered many casualties. Only three remain, along with Captain Ben. To make matters worse, the stables are guarded by a small Autoch detachment led by a Dark Knight. The only way into the stable's wide-open doors is directly through them.

Jet does not pause. He charges right at the Knight and engages him. The rest of the group follows closely behind, though another Panorum soldier is downed before he can reach his enemy. The fighting is the fiercest the group has faced so far, but the Autochs' skills with their swords are lacking compared to the survivors. One-by-one, the Autoch are cut down.

Jet is having more difficulty with the Knight, however. Every attack he levies against him is deftly parried, and now he finds himself on the defensive. He blocks an overhead attack from the Knight, but the sheer force of it knocks his blade down to the ground. He recoils backwards in anticipation of the Knight's upward swing, but cannot avoid the point of his enemy's sword. It cuts shallowly through his right cheek, misses his eye by an inch, and continues through his brow and forehead. He screams in pain and falls onto his back as blood drips into his eyes, rendering them momentarily useless.

The Knight is moving in to finish his work when Skyler and her last surviving Aurelican soldier set upon him. The two briefly put the Knight on his back foot as he struggles to repel their surprise attack, yet it only takes a few moments for the Knight to collect himself and refocus. With a couple controlled dodges, he catches both Skyler and her Aurelican compatriot overextended. The Knight kicks Skyler's feet out from under her, causing her to fall to the ground and hit her head, then plunges his sword through the other Aurelican's chest. Wasting no time, he pulls his sword out and swings it down at Skyler, only to have his strike slapped away at the last moment by Aris.

With Skyler still dazed, Aris stands alone against the Knight. Angry, the Knight swings his sword as hard as he can at Aris, who catches the blade with his own. With their swords crossed, the Knight presses down upon Aris, forcing Aris's blade toward his own neck and driving him to one knee. Just as Aris's strength is about to fail him, the Knight spins around as several gunshots ring out from behind him. The Knight manages to block two, leaving another seventeen to catch him directly in the chest. The rest of the Autoch squad has been killed, and every remaining survivor has fired upon him. The Knight releases his sword and slumps face-first to the ground.

Ben and Azen rush over to pick up Aris and Skyler respectively. Ben grabs Aris's hand and smiles. "You can't die yet, Aris. You still have to protect me."

Skyler puts her hand on Aris's soldier. "Protect us all. As we shall protect him," she adds to Ben's statement, looking into Aris's eyes. "For we all depend upon each other for survival."

"Our survival depends on us ever getting out of this mess," Azen interjects anxiously.

"Indeed," Ben agrees. "Grab a saddle from inside the stable and choose your steed wisely. We ride for the Horventi Plain."

***

Not far from the stables is Izedar Dumelor. He is making short work of the surviving Panorum in a compound when another Dark Knight approaches him. "My Lord Izedar. Autoch inform me Sir Undar and his battalion have been eradicated."

"A desperate attempt by the Panorum to abandon their kin and save themselves," Izedar sneers. "I expect nothing less from the descendants of cowards."

"That's not the end of it, my Lord. It, apparently, was a force mixed with other northerners, led by an Ithoran Inpyrian Knight."

"Impossible." Izedar says out loud to himself. "Take the rest of my acolytes with you. Grab horses from the stable and hunt them down. Several high-value foreigners may yet still remain amongst that group. It is imperative that they are eliminated. I will meet you at the valley floor."

"It will be done, my Lord."

***

Back at the stable, each survivor picks a horse and mounts up. Once everyone is ready, Ben gives the command. "Ride now! To the golden plain! Let no evil block you! For you are all a light that has cut through great darkness and, as long you hold true to your purpose, you will never be burnt out, in life or in death! Hyah!"

He kicks his horse, and it breaks into a gallop. The others launch into a charge quickly to follow him. They race out of the barn and weave through the trees at breakneck speed. Autoch fire upon them, but cannot hit their moving targets, and any who attempt to move into the riders' path are promptly trampled.

The escapees reach the ungated entrance to the city and take a sharp right to rejoin the Orus Pass along the northern bank of the Alcyon River. A long descent awaits them through the mountains.

With the night sky now overhead, the city's burning light slowly disappears from their rear view.

23

Fractured Lines

It's a gray day in Aurelia City. A soft and steady rain pitter-patters on the upper city marble. Little streams of rainwater roll down the city's hillside. A single blanket cloud covers the entire sky, blocking out what would be the midday sun. The city is active, despite the weather. Businesses continue to operate, and citizens simply move with a little more urgency to their destinations. The White Wall gate is open, and the Elysian Gate Bridge remains lowered. Farmers and traders, dressed in ponchos and with coverings over their goods, flow in and out of the city.

It is truly a mundane day in the kingdom—that is, until a single rider approaches at top speed. Apart from his epaulettes, the rider looks the same as any citizen. The white feathered decorations on his shoulders indicate his purpose. He is a member of the Interkingdom Messenger Company, or IMC for short. To be riding at such a pace indicates whatever letter he bears has been sent with the highest of importance.

The rider weaves through the crowded White Wall gate courtyard and perseveres through muddy footing to the upper city. Aurelicans jump out of his way left and right all the way to the royal palace. At the end of the plaza, the rider dismounts and hands a sealed message to a robed emissary who has come out to meet him. Once the message is handed off, the messenger relaxes, remounts his horse, and slowly trots away.

The emissary doesn't keep the same level of urgency as the messenger, but does walk at a brisk pace to the throne room, where King Jackson sits with his royal council around the end of the main wooden table. The king has appointed nine members in total to the council, although only five are present. The present council members are Sir Chase Seever, Lady Aly Bentha, Lady Tilla Nef, Sir Trenton Ervis, and General Ella Macintyre. All members of the council are middle-aged except for Lady Tilla and Sir Trenton, whose lack of experience is forgiven due to their high regard at the Inpyrium.

When the emissary enters, Jackson pays him no mind. He expects the emissary to lay the message on the table and leave. Instead, the emissary hands the scroll directly to him and whispers in his ear. "My King, this message was sent with top priority."

The council's conversation has stopped, and all eyes are fixed on Jackson. The King takes the message, inspects the insignia on the seal, and gives an affirming nod to the emissary. "Dark have been these days of late. With every passing moment, evil casts an invisible shadow upon our lands, obfuscating our kingdom's future. Ithorans invade Zyber, pillaging and enslaving as they march; Valendi assault the New Baylands, only to make an irrational peace at the brink of destruction; and now, a messenger arrives at the royal palace, bearing a letter sealed with the insignia of our informant in Belfhen... Let us all hope that the contents of this message are not what I think they are."

King Jackson breaks the seal and reads the letter briefly to himself. Once he is finished, he slowly sets it down on the table and stares off to the right, looking through the raindrop-covered windows and out to the ocean. "Woe is me; for I shall rule in the dark when my forebears have seen nothing but light."

Jackson turns to the emissary and hands him the message. "Send word of this treachery to all of the northern kingdoms and the Inpyrium, recall our garrison from Eastfort immediately, and get a ship out to Admiral Tyler to inform him that he is to engage any Baylander vessel that attempts to break our blockade, which will be set in line with our ground forces."

The emissary nods and strides out of the room. King Jackson directs his attention back to the council. "General Macintyre, you will command our entire army south to halt the Baylander invasion into the Freelands. Sir Trenton and Lady Tilla will join you as your two top Inpyrian officers. Lady Aly and Sir Chase will remain here to provide me council and protection until my full royal guard returns from the east. You two will also need to help me orchestrate a program for Freelander refugees."

King Jackson then focuses his eyes directly on the General. "I have the utmost confidence King Venden will protect your left flank, whether they declare war against the Baylanders or not. You must focus all of your efforts on holding our line together and limiting our casualties. Bend, but do not break. They will outnumber us, but we have the defensive advantage. This is not a war we can win through audacious attacks. We must outlast our enemy."

"I will send word to our generals to rally the army here at once," Ella replies seriously.

The over-forty-year-old general exudes a stern confidence in her mannerisms. She has seen enough winters to count herself as one of the most experienced in the Aurelican army. War of this magnitude, however, has not been seen by any current soldier. She will have to rely on her training to guide the army properly through this crisis.

"Good. March as soon as you are ready. Council adjourned."

The council members stand, give slight bows, and make for the exit. Jackson remains seated, staring blankly ahead and stroking his beard. No actual planning is occurring, but the weight of the world pins him to his chair. The room is dead silent save for the sound of light raindrops smacking against the windows. Time passes, but the King does not break his position.

If Aurelica falls, the world shall surely follow.

24

Shattered Future

Captain Ben raises his right arm. "Hold!" he commands, slowing his steed.

The horses have been trotting for hours through the night. There is just enough light from the stars and a crescent moon to give the group sufficient visibility. On their left runs the Alcyon River, along with the Alcyon Railroad tracks. On their right lies a small town comprised of wooden and stone buildings. The area is narrow, with the Orus mountains flanking them in every direction.

Ben raises his voice. "We make camp here. That inn over there should have food and drink, along with enough beds, since this place looks to be already evacuated. We will need a watch up full-time. Keep your horses saddled. We leave at even the slightest hint of an enemy presence."

Jet, now sporting a thin scar up his right cheek and brow, rides up to Ben. "Is it wise to linger here? There will be time to rest when we are out of the mountains."

"We don't have much of a choice. Mill Town is the only settlement on the Orus Pass between Starlinden and the Horventi Plains. The horses are fatigued, and many of us have gone without any real food, drink, or sleep for days. The army, of course, will not catch us. Our only threat is stolen calvary, which would require the enemy to be targeting us specifically."

"It didn't stop them before."

"True..." Ben looks around at the remaining ten soldiers, including he and Jet. "But we were also much greater in number then. Judging by the fact that this town is empty, the word of the enemy invasion is out. I think we are no longer of strategic importance."

"That is, if you don't know the contents of our group," Jet replies, looking at Azen and Skyler, who walk toward the inn.

Ben and Jet dismount and tie their horses at the side of the inn. "Let us hope they do not," Ben replies.

Argand lamps line the tables and walls inside the inn's bottom floor, which is walled and floored entirely of stone compared to its second-floor wooden exterior. The lamps give the room a dim orange tint; enough visibility to see, but still a dark feel. Acquiring food and drink is easy, as the tables have been left with both resting upon them, as if people had vanished into thin air during a vibrant night in the town. The group wastes little time to scarf down the leftovers without a word said to each other.

Once everyone has quenched their appetite, Azen speaks openly to the group. "When we reach the end of the Orus Pass, our paths will be limitless. Might I suggest—or rather offer, for those of you without direction—that you come with me back to my capital city of Dunhaven. I will ensure King Venden will treat you all as his most honored guests, as that is what you deserve after this debacle."

Ben answers. "Your offer is most generous, Commander Azen. I am afraid that after the fall of Starlinden, the Panorum here have nowhere else to go. All of our nearby towns are connected via our capital. They cannot be accessed from the plain without great hardship."

Skyler then speaks. "Your city is on the way home for the rest of us as well. We would all be honored to experience the hospitality of your great halls."

The group nods in agreement, except for Jet. "Unfortunately, our journey together ends at Eswen Station," Jet laments, referring to the small Horventi town at the entrance of the Orus Pass. "I must ride to the Inpyrium immediately to report all the details of our ill-fated journey. There are forces at work here beyond armies and kingdoms. I fear all of Amoria is caught in this shadow."

Ben stands and looks at Jet. "Then it is imperative you reach your destination, unravel the mysterious web of our enemy, and avenge our kin who have fallen in its wake." Jet rises from his chair and gives a reassuring nod back to Ben. Ben then addresses the entire group. "Now, get some rest. It'll be a half-hour watch for each of us, and I will take the first. We ride at first light tomorrow."

With that, everyone heads upstairs to the now-unoccupied beds in the inn. Sleep comes easy for the survivors thanks to their exhaustion. Even the trauma of the past few days cannot abate their extreme tiredness. The only sounds that permeate the air are the rapids of the Alcyon, the crickets, and the occasional hoot of a distant owl.

Indeed, it is just as dawn begins to breach the night sky from the east that Jet awakens startled. He looks around his room, where Callathar Ejyn and Devden Skip sleep peacefully in separate beds, Cal with the sheets hardly covering her, and the husky Skip face-down with a heavy snore. The sounds outside the inn remain steady.

However, despite Jet's eyes' reassurances, a disturbance persists in his mind. Still fully dressed in case of a need of a hasty exit, he moves out of his room and down through the inn's bottom floor. He gently pushes aside the wooden saloon doors, which creak loudly in response. Across the road and to the east, the Panorum soldier supposedly on watch lays flat on her back. Jet looks both directions, seeing nothing out of the ordinary, before crossing quietly over to the soldier. He reaches her and shakes her to wake her up. It takes only a second for him to realize why she does not stir—her throat has been cut.

Jet jerks his head back up in fear. Still nothing.

He scampers softly back to inn. Once inside, he breaks into a full sprint into Captain Ben's room. His bursting into the room wakes Ben, Aris, and Skyler, who have been sound asleep there. "The watcher has been murdered. We need to leave now!" Jet whispers with urgency.

The three erupt from their beds and move for the door while Jet wakes the other two rooms. Everyone is already dressed to leave, allowing them to gather themselves quickly and head to their horses out back.

A Dark Knight has beaten them to their destination. The morning sky gives Jet enough light to see what the Knight is about to do—he has drawn his sword to cut the horses' throats. Jet draws his pistol and fires on him to stop him. The Knight spins and parries the bullet with his sword at the last second. The sound of the shot echoes all the way up off the mountain walls.

"Get to your horses!" Jet yells as he breaks into a sprint directly at the Knight.

The Knight shoots once at him with his own pistol, but Jet blocks it with his blade. The Knight, realizing he is facing a fellow Inpyrian, quickly holsters his gun and prepares for a duel. Jet instead launches himself at the Knight's hips and tackles him to the ground, causing the Knight to drop his sword backwards. The Knight kicks Jet off of him and spins back to grab his weapon, but when he turns, Jet is no longer in front of him. Instead, he has rushed off and mounted his steed.

Jet kicks, and his horse breaks into a gallop to catch up with the others, who have already left. The Knight breaks into a run up the town to where he left his own mount. Four other Dark Knights pass him on their horses as he moves.

The chase is on.

"It's only a few mountains further before it's downhill all the way to the valley!" Ben yells to the group. "Do not pace your steeds. Hopefully, there will be a train in station at Eswen. If not, we can split up."

"Captain!" Skyler yells. "Behind us!"

At a gallop, the five Dark Knights gain on the group. The sound of gunfire precipitates the sound of bullets whizzing past the group's ears. "Return fire!" Ben orders.

The more skilled riders—more explicitly, the two surviving Horventi and Panorum—along with Jet, fire back on their enemy. Jet uses his pistol, while the others use their rifles. Eventually, one of the bullets catches the Panorum soldier's horse, causing it to stumble over and throw its rider off.

"Johner!" Ben swings his horse around and rides over to aid the last of his command.

"Ben! No!" Azen yells at him, but Ben's mind is made up. He isn't leaving anyone behind.

Jet turns back to aid him. The others continue forward.

With only 200 feet separating him and the charging Knights, Ben reaches the fallen Panorum soldier, extends his arm, and, in one swift move, pulls him onto the back of his horse. The Knights fire a volley at him, but Jet rides in between them and parries the two bullets that would have hit their mark. With the Panorum soldier rescued, the three burst back west with the enemy practically breathing down their necks.

***

Eventually, the rest of the group reaches the final western slopes of the Orus range. The vast Horventi Plains stretch infinitely to the north and south. The morning mountain shadow still covers the plains' eastern section, but the western section reflects the golden light of the sun. Far in the distance, the great city of Dunhaven basks in sunlight, just off of the tip of the mountains' shadow. If one looks hard enough, they may even be able to see Aurelica on the edge of the horizon, but there is no time to take in the view. They ride onward with what speed their horses can still muster.

Ben's group arrives at the same point a few minutes later. With escape now in plain view, the soldier Ben saved speaks above the sounds of hooves clattering. "Captain, your courage through this has saved us all. We are perm—" A bullet catches him straight through the back of his head, cutting off his sentence before he can finish. His grip around Ben fails, and he slumps off of the horse to the ground.

Great sorrow fills Ben. The soldier's death solidifies his complete failure to protect his people in his first role as captain in the army. Not one Panorum remains—he couldn't save even a single one of them.

At the front, a Horventi rider reaches Eswen Station with the others a few hundred meters behind. The town is entirely comprised of two-story wooden buildings in a five-by-five block radius, with an open-air train station on the northern Alcyon riverbank. Just south of the station is a wide and unraised wooden bridge. This junction is the last bridged crossing of Alcyon until Dunhaven, making it a key Horventi and Panorum trading outpost. The main train is not in the station, but there is still a smaller three-car train available. Known as a missile train, it's the fastest type of train ever invented, designed to transport either goods or people at top speeds. What gives the train its name is how it starts—via a black-powder explosion like a cannon.

The rider heads straight for it, dismounts his horse, and begins preparations for launch. Moments later, the rest of the group arrives. Azen calls to the rider who has positioned himself at the launching station. "What's the status of the train, Jeffen?"

"There's coal already loaded, and the powder-launcher is packed tight. We can take off as soon as everyone is aboard."

Azen looks back at Jet and Ben charging into town with the five Dark Knights at their heels. As they reach the plains, Jet turns right sharply to head north, pulling two riders with him in tow.

"No time to waste, then," he says as he dismounts. "Give Ben cover fire as he approaches!"

The group opens fire, and Ben's three pursuing Knights spread out their formation to avoid the shots. The maneuver delays them and gives Ben enough time to reach the group safely.

"Let's go!" Azen yells, still firing down at the riders.

The survivors dismount and turn to hop on the train. Aris, who is closest to Jeffen, is only twenty feet away when a Dark Knight fires on the powder launcher. The bullet punctures a hole straight through the back of the metal box, causing the slightest spark as it enters the powder. The powder is ignited and, with the structural integrity of the launcher comprised, the entire device explodes. Jeffen is incinerated instantly, and the back two cars of the metal train shatter into shrapnel. The fiery blast must be at least 200 feet high. Everyone is thrown from their feet.

Aris rises, dazed, to see their escape plan in pieces and flames. He turns back to his horse, which lies dead on the ground, caught by metal fragments in the blast. Ben's horse has also been struck down.

"Aris! Take my hand!" Skyler yells to him from her horse. She grabs him and pulls him up onto her mount.

"Ben needs a ride as well!" Aris yells out to the group, who have all re-mounted.

Azen turns back to grab him, but Ben has another idea. "Go! I will delay them to ensure your escape. Aris, your duty to protect me is complete. It is now my turn to finally save you all."

Azen yells back, "Nonsense, Captain! You are coming with us!"

"No! I am still in command, Commander, and I will be damned if I let the rest of you die as well! Now go, before it's too late!"

The Knights are heading directly for them. The window to save Ben is gone. Azen grunts in anguished frustration and turns his horse away. Cal and Skip do the same. Aris's eyes water as they take one last look at the brave Captain. Ben turns to face the dark riders, and Skyler's horse rears as she pulls reigns.

With the last of the Eastfort survivors riding off, Ben stands alone against the three Knights. However, they have no plans of stopping for him. He is not who they pursue. Ben figures as much. As soon as he is as confident in his aim as he can be, he fires at the horse to his left and then to his right. Then he dives at the final horse closest to him. The Knights are unable to defend against the low gunfire, and the two outside horses are gunned down in front of him. In his dive, Ben uses his sword to clip the legs of the central horse, which causes it to tumble head-over-heels and sends its rider flying past him.

All three Knights arise slowly after their heavy falls. Ben rushes to engage the closest Knight before the others can reach him, but he is no match for even one of them. The Knight parries, with some difficulty, Ben's flurry of vengeful strikes, eventually crossing their swords.

It is at this moment another Knight reaches and swings at him. Ben parries and pushes the Knight backwards. The third Knight arrives, and Ben parries his strike as well, only to have the first Knight thrust her sword through his back.

Ben freezes while the Knight pulls her sword back out of him. He yells and swings wildly at the Knight who stabbed him. The Knight easily dodges, then slashes down through the left side of his neck.

Ben falls to his knees and drops his sword. He briefly covers his neck with his left hand to restrict the bleeding, but then takes his hand off the wound and looks at it. There is so much blood he cannot even see his own skin. Struggling to breathe, he lets his hand fall to his side. He looks out past his assailant to the horizon to see four horses riding away in the distance, now glowing in the morning sun.

His last strength fades away, and he collapses face-first into the dirt.

Made in the USA
Monee, IL
23 July 2023